# 所寶惟賢 奕伯文物鑒賞

*A Sage's Respect for Artistic Treasures*
*—An Exhibition of Uncle Shuang's Collection*

97.11.14-97.12.14

開放時間
每日上午十時至下午六時
國定例假日照常開放

展覽地點
國立歷史博物館四樓
台北市南海路四九號

主辦單位
國立歷史博物館
NATIONAL MUSEUM OF HISTORY

協辦單位
寒舍股份有限公司

所寶惟賢與伯文物鑒賞

卷一 玉冊

## 所寶惟賢

「聖人養萬民而不能不賴賢之時亮天工。是以周公躬吐握之勞，故有囿空之隆，齊桓設庭燎之禮，故有匡合之功。寰區至廣也，生民至眾也，以一人之心智耳目御之，其敝精勞神而迄無成功，亦不待燭照數計而龜卜矣。自古賢王勞于求賢，逸於得人，然得人始逸而求賢則勞，毋論求之不以道，得之不以實，所得非其人，所求非其賢，而天下之萬民，不可以一日而不養。為君難，蓋誠乎其難矣！」（《清高宗御製文初集》卷一）

取自《明清帝后寶璽》

# 目錄

# Contents

## Volume 1

# 國立歷史博物館館長序

吳先旺先生是一位成功的企業家，也是一位有高尚品味的文物鑑賞家，更是一位熱情的收藏家。他對文物的喜好是天生的。早年因生活貧困與失學，根本不知文物為何物；但對於美的東西有一種發自內心的強烈親近感。及至事業有成後，他對許多物質性的東西，難免以成本效益的角度來衡量，唯獨對於藝術品及文物之收藏，完全不考慮任何現實利益。特別是每當看到精美的藝術品或文物，流落在國外，更往往會不計代價，非要將之「買」回來不可！

吳先生是位性情中人，朋友都稱他「爽伯」，他也喜歡大家這樣稱呼他。他對文物有一種獨特的興趣與執著。所謂興趣，是指接觸的範圍廣泛而多元；執著，是指非高品質與自己真正喜歡者絕不收藏。他收藏文物二十餘年，足跡遍及世界各地，收藏品類共十餘項，其中以玉石器佔大多數。這些眾多的玉石器中，許多是流落國外的清代皇室文物，幾乎件件都是絕世精品，不僅具有高度的藝術審美價值，更是重要的歷史文物資料。它們既見證了十九世紀西方帝國主義者掠奪文物之滄桑，也提供了十七世紀以來傳統工藝美術發展演進的實存物證。

傳統藝術與文物，是歷史變遷的時空膠囊，它們反映過去人們對生命的關照與生活之體驗，是人們心靈實踐的結晶。國立歷史博物館敬重吳先旺先生，長年來對蒐羅流落海外中華文物不遺餘力之貢獻，同時感佩其始終樂意提供社會大眾欣賞，與學術界人士比較研究的無私精神，因此特別規劃此項展覽，除展出吳先生個人的珍藏，也獲得許多收藏界同好共襄盛舉。相信這些珍貴的收藏與如此難得的展覽，一定可以拓展國人對傳統文物的欣賞視野，謹此誠摯邀請大家共同分享指教。

國立歷史博物館館長

黃永川　謹識

as well as the treasures of Mr. Wu Xian-Wang's collection. We hope that these precious collections in this unique exhibition will expand the horizons of our compatriots in terms of the appreciation of traditional cultural artifacts. I hereby invite everyone to appreciate this exhibition and look forward to your valuable comments.

**Huang Yong-Chuan**
**Director**
**National Museum of History**

# Introduction

Mr. Wu Xian-Wang is not only a successful businessman; he is also a sophisticated appreciator of cultural artifacts and a passionate collector. His love of cultural artifacts is in his character. In his early years, he had no knowledge of such things, having been brought up in poverty and lacked schooling, but he had an intense attraction for beautiful things that came from deep inside his heart. After succeeding in business, he couldn't help but view material things from the viewpoint of cost effectiveness, but practical benefits were never taken into consideration in his collection of art and cultural artifacts. Whenever he saw an exquisite artwork or cultural artifact that had ended up in another country, he would have to buy it, no matter the price, in order to bring it back to its rightful home.

Mr. Wu is a person who expresses his emotions directly, and his friends even call him "Mr. Frank." He likes it when people call him that. He has his own kind of interest and insistence as far as artifacts are concerned. The interest is a broad and diverse one, and his insistence is never to collect objects that are not of high quality or that he does not truly like. In his more than 20 years of collecting, he has been all over the world in pursuit of more than 10 types of artifacts, of which jade constitutes the majority. Much of this large amount of jade is Qing Dynasty imperial artifacts that have been dispersed to other countries, and almost every piece is a historical treasure. They not only have a high level of artistic value, but are also important historical items. They testify to the plundering of cultural artifacts by the Western imperial powers of the nineteenth century and they provide hard evidence of the evolution of traditional artistic techniques from the seventeenth century onward.

Traditional art and cultural artifacts are time capsules that allow us to view the changes of history. They reflect the concern for life and the experience of living of peoples of the past. They are crystallizations of those people's spirit and practice. The National Museum of History respects Mr. Wu Xian-Wang's unflagging contributions in the collection of Chinese artifacts that have found their way to various foreign countries over the years. We also admire the unselfishness of his constant willingness to provide them for appreciation by society at large and for study by scholars. We have therefore, specially planned this exhibition, which presents artifacts from many other collectors,

# 外雙溪故宮博物院的鄰居——爽伯

五洲製藥董事長吳先旺先生，三十多年前，以「足爽」起家，大家暱稱為「爽伯」。爽伯好古愛奇，他的文物收藏看來質材不拘，非常隨性，但不外乎中華文物，古今兼備；可是細究起來，還是有一個主軸，就是他喜歡買前清故宮流失海外的遺珍。無怪乎阿爽伯擇鄰而居，住在外雙溪故宮博物院附近的透天厝，藉地利之便，可以多親近故宮文物，培養眼力。

二十世紀八〇、九〇年代，台灣的經濟實力大增，歐洲、美國等地的中國文物回流成為風潮。長久以來，爽伯通過不同的管道，包括拍賣公司以及國內外的經紀人尋寶、掌眼。爽伯的藏品中器物與書畫兼備，然先秦禮器付闕，古玉二、三事而已，雅俗共賞的文玩成為大宗。書畫卷軸為人稱道的，有乾隆皇帝親筆所書〈登岱山御筆詩長卷〉，內容紀錄乾隆皇帝登泰山時所詠佳句。秦皇漢武、歷代皇帝都有上泰山祭天，為國祈福的傳統。長卷前並鈐〈五福五代堂古稀天子寶〉、〈八徵耄念之寶〉兩方大璽。乾隆時儒臣張若靄〈摹唐寅折枝牡丹卷〉前後登載於清皇室書畫著錄《石渠寶笈》初編，與嘉慶年間所編的《石渠寶笈三編》，鑑藏璽印一應俱全。〈清世宗朝服立像〉則是難得一見的雍正皇帝大幅全身肖像，保存情況完好。

爽伯收藏的文玩，包括青銅、鎏金百寶嵌、犀角、竹木、紫檀、白玉、黃玉、青玉、翡翠、水晶、窯瓷等各類質材。製成筆筒、硯屏、文具匣扁、香爐、香筒、圓雕動物、神獸、人物、如意、扳指、鼻煙壺、飲食器用、仿古禮器、犧尊擺件等，往往器底或器座上還鐫刻銘文、評定等第，或乾隆宸翰、或嘉慶皇帝、光緒皇帝的款識，琳瑯滿目，足證為清宮故物。璽印藏品中有白芙蓉、田黃等價值不菲的印材，也有精工雕鏤的嘉慶皇帝玉質閒章，頗有可觀。碧玉盝頂形蟠螭紐印璽組「嘉慶御筆」、「所寶惟賢」、「所其無逸」三件，玉筋篆體的朱文、白文配搭，一起放置在質樸的檀木盒內。「所寶惟賢」語出《尚書》，可以引伸的意思是敬重寶者就是「賢」人，無怪乎雍正皇帝、乾隆皇帝也都各有一方「所寶惟賢」印。史博館楊式昭女史即以此為展覽定名，是神來之筆。

蒐購文物，起始都是以嗜好之癖、耳目之玩為事，然而一路下來所費不貲，心境上會有轉折。聖經上說：「你的錢在哪裡，你的心就在哪裡。」撇開古物能保值或者增值不談，收藏家往往會因為金錢上的投資，轉而為精神上的全神投入，不單就古物本身，古物背後聚散流轉的歷史，都想掌握與瞭解，無形中開闊了視野，增長了知識。

孟子曾經對齊宣王說過：「獨樂樂，與人樂樂，孰樂？」齊宣王曰：「不若與人。」與大家同樂，就是一種喜樂。先人手澤，傳世古物，重在發揚，才能發揮它的賞鑑價值。爽伯走過七十人生漫長路，卻一點也不世故，個性十分阿沙力，今服膺先哲之言，願與大家分享他的珍藏。由家人選出藏品中具代表性者一百餘事，假國立歷史博物館展出，以寄文雅之娛，並藉此祝福他耆碩康強。

震旦藝術博物館館長

張臨生

Dynasty emperor such as Qianlong, Jiaqing, or Guangxu. There are many examples of these, and it proves that they came from the Qing Dynasty Imperial Palace. The imperial seals in the collection include those made of precious materials such as white furong stone and yellow tianhuang stone. There are also gorgeous seals with exquisite carving work that were used by Emperor Jiaqing. There is a three-piece set of dark green jade roof-shaped imperial seals carved with coiled chi-dragons, placed in a sandalwood case. One of the inscriptions, a line taken from Shangshu, means that the person who respects these artistic treasures is a sage. Emperor Yongzheng and Emperor Qianlong also had seals with identical inscriptions. Hence it is pure genius of Mrs. Grace Shi-Zhao Tu of the National Museum of History to use it as the name of this exhibition.

Collecting artifacts starts out as a hobby, or just as something to appreciate. Then, as the expenses start to add up, there is a psychological shift. The Bible states that "Where your money is, there is where your heart is." Putting aside the argument that ancient artifacts maintain or increase in value, collectors often change from just investing money to investing their whole energy. They wish to understand the stories behind the artifacts, and they imperceptibly expand their horizons and accumulate knowledge.

Mencius once said to King Xuan of Qi, "Which is the more pleasant - to enjoy music by yourself alone, or to enjoy it with others?" The king replied, "To enjoy it with others." Sharing your joy with others is a joy in itself. Our ancestors made records and passed down treasures. Only by letting others enjoy them can their true value be developed. Uncle Shuang has seen over 70 years of this world, but he is not worldly at all. He is generous by nature, and he remembers the words of the ancient philosopher that told him to share his treasures. The exhibition at the National Museum of History consists of more than 100 pieces selected by his family to represent the elegance of his collection. This exhibition also serves as a wish for a wise and generous man to live a long and healthy life.

*Chang Lin-Sheng*

**Chang Lin-Sheng**
**Director**
**Aurora Art Museum**

# The National Palace Museum's Neighbor Uncle Shuang

Thirty years ago, Mr. Wu Xian-Wang, Chairman of U.C. Pharma, started out his career with "Zu Shuang" (meaning "Happy Feet") foot cream, and the nickname "Uncle Shuang" stuck with him after that. Uncle Shuang has a passion for ancient artwork, and his artifact collection, while consisting of Chinese artifacts only, is eclectic and not limited to a certain type or era. However, if you look closely, there is a main thread, which is that he likes to buy Qing Dynasty treasures that made their way into overseas collections from the Imperial Palace at Beijing. It is no wonder that Uncle Shuang chooses to live in a house on the slope beside Chih-te Garden to the right of the National Palace Museum at Wai-shuan-hsi. It has been very convenient for him to be close to the artifacts of the Imperial Palace, allowing him to cultivate a good eye.

Taiwan's economic power grew in the 1980's and 1990's, making possible the trend of Chinese artifacts flowing back from Europe and America. For a long time, Uncle Shuang has been searching for treasures through many different channels such as auctions and through Chinese and foreign agents. His collection includes both artifacts and paintings, lacking in pre-Qin ritual objects and scant in ancient jades while rich and exuberant in scholar's objects that are appreciated by the refined eye and the common taste alike. Among the calligraphy and painting scrolls, the most noteworthy is one personally made by Qing Dynasty Emperor Qianlong which is a poem recording an ascent of Mount Tai. It was a tradition for emperors, since ancient times, to climb Mount Tai to present offerings to heaven and pray for the gods' blessings on behalf of the kingdom. There are two large imperial seals on the front of the scroll. A painting by scholarly courtier Zhang Ruo-Ai of the Qianlong era, which was collected in two Qing Dynasty anthologies, is stamped with all the necessary imperial seals. There is also a rare full-length portrait of Emperor Yongzheng that has been well preserved.

The scholar's objects collected by Uncle Shuang are of all types of material such as bronze, gilt bronze with gems inlay, rhino horn, bamboo and wood, red sandalwood, white jade, yellow jade, grayish green jade, jadeite, crystal, and porcelain. These materials have been formed into brush holders, screens for inkstones, stationery trays, censers, incense holders, sculptures of animals, mythical beasts, and human figures, ru-yi scepters, thumb rings, snuff bottles, eating and drinking vessels, replicas of ancient ritual vessels for decoration. There usually can be found a carved inscription on the bottom or the wood base of the objects that marked its assessment rating or personal seal of a Qing

# 寒舍主人序

民國七十四年秋天，我與人稱「爽伯」的吳先旺董事長，巧遇在台北士林一間頗負盛名的園藝店。當年，我們因雅好收藏盆景而結識，經常一邊品茗飲酒，一邊交換植栽心得，愜意自在，不亦樂乎！有一天，先旺兄神秘而興奮地從懷中取出一件古玉向我討教，我也坦率客觀地就材質、雕工加以分析解說。從此，我倆亦師亦友，教學相長，一路走來竟已二十餘年。吳董事長不僅是「寒舍」的常客，也成為台灣古董界家喻戶曉的傳奇人物。

談到爽伯的奇人奇事，常為大家所津津樂道。尤其是他人生起伏與創業過程的堅毅奮鬥，從機車學徒到創立製藥王國，從小學肄業到藝術藏家，我們不得不對吳董事長感到激勵與欽佩。誠如他在電視廣告中的那句名言：「有好的產品才有好的商標，有好的商標才有百年企業」。他把對事業研發的那份堅持，也投入在藝術品的收藏研究上，求知若渴，虛心請教；眼光獨到，收藏精準。如果說在台灣的藝術史，洪通先生是一位素人畫家，那麼吳先旺先生，可以算是一位成功的「素人藏家」了！

此次歷史博物館舉辦「所寶惟賢──爽伯文物鑑賞展」，將吳先旺先生二十年來的收藏，以及藏家友人之珍寶，共同挑選了百件精品，首度公開亮相，從宮廷玉器乃至田黃古玩，件件都可算是國寶級藏品。這些藝術品以今天國際拍賣市場的行情來估量，真是非常可觀，我常在想，爽伯當年若是把這些錢花在名車珠寶上，可有今天豐富的回報嗎？不過每件藏品都是他的心肝寶貝，都是難以割愛的。欣逢吳董事長七十大壽，特此祝賀這位古董界的老頑童，老當益壯，福壽雙全！

寒舍主人

蔡辰洋

could not bear to part with any of them. On the occasion of Chairman Wu's seventieth birthday, I would like to wish this playful gentleman of the collecting world an especially enjoyable second youth filled with both fortune and longevity!

**Tsai Chen-Yang**
**Owner of My Humble House**

# Foreword

On an autumn's day in 1985, I had a chance meeting at a very famous gardening store with Chairman Wu Xian-Wang, whom I and many others call "Uncle Shuang". In that year, we made a friendship because we both enjoyed collecting potted plants. We often talked about horticulture over tea or wine, contented and relaxed in each other's good company! One day, Xian-Wang mysteriously and excitedly produced a piece of ancient jade from his breast pocket and asked me about it. I gave him an honest and objective analysis of its material and workmanship. Since then, we two friends have been each other's teacher and student as we have studied together for over 20 years. Chairman Wu was not only a regular visitor to My Humble House Art Gallery; he also became a legendary figure well known throughout the antique collecting world in Taiwan.

I often get excited when speaking of Uncle Shuang's amazing achievements, especially concerning his determined struggle throughout the ups and downs of his life and career. He advanced from being a motorcycle repair apprentice to the founder of a pharmaceutical empire and from a boy who didn't finish elementary school to an art collector. We can't help but be inspired by and feel admiration for Chairman Wu. It's just like he says in that television commercial: "A good brand comes from a good product, and a hundred-year enterprise is built on a good brand." He took his persistence in business research and development and injected it into artwork collection and research. He has a thirst for knowledge and the modesty to seek consultation. In his collecting, he has shown his unique taste and perfectionism. If, in the history of art in Taiwan, Hong Tong is considered a natural painter, then Wu Xian-Wang can be considered a successful natural collector!

This "A Sage's Respect for Artistic Treasures — An Exhibition of Uncle Shuang's Collection" held by the National Museum of History will display to the public for the first time 100 pieces selected from Wu Xian-Wang's 20-year collection as well as treasures from fellow collectors. From jade implements of the imperial court to Tianhuang studio curios, each and every piece can be considered a national treasure. I often wonder whether, if the value of these artworks on the international auction market were to be estimated, Uncle Shuang's investment would turn out to have been more profitable than if he had spent his money on classic cars or jewelry. But all of these pieces are the apple of his eye, and he

# 一塊錢的麵，我想了五十五年

五十五年前，那時我剛從南部上台北當機車行的「黑手」，一個月薪水沒多少，但因為家裡還要用錢，我一毛錢都捨不得多花。當時的同事、後來的台益機車行老闆劉鴻儒（現任台北市機車商業同業公會理事長），請我吃了一碗陽春麵，那時，我在故鄉窮到連飯都沒得吃，這碗陽春麵，珍貴得像個奇蹟。

那是很多年前的故事了。在「歷史博物館」的「所寶惟賢」收藏展前夕，為什麼我又想起了那碗麵？

因為我又想起了「感謝」的滋味。在我這「窮鬼翻身」打拚的一生中，幾乎所有美好的事，都得來不易，凡是得到的，都要感謝很多人成全。

這次因為我過七十歲生日，兒子宗明希望幫我辦一個有意義的生日，他邀請收藏界的朋友為我舉行收藏聯展，也讓我想起「感謝」的滋味。

記得展前，歷史博物館館長黃永川先生和副館長高玉珍女士，帶著史博館的研究人員、專家學者到我家看收藏，到了之後，我雖是主人，卻得退到一邊，不得發表意見，要讓專家有獨立的空間專注觀察和判斷。我遠遠看著學者們拿著尺仔細的又量又記，專注的討論，一付嚴格把關的樣子，我心裡升起了敬重的感覺，「啊！人家這就是專業。」他們這樣慎重的看待我這些年收藏的古文物，那時我的感覺，就是「感謝」。

這次展覽，還有一位重要推手，就是「寒舍」蔡辰洋先生。古文物收藏，他是帶我入門的前輩，讓我開了眼、看懂什麼是好東西。這次收藏展前，他也到我家來幫忙過濾展品，蔡先生已經是古董界的前輩，但極慎重和愛惜羽毛，一看就看了六個小時，還取笑我說：「爽伯仔，你收這麼多，是要開古董店哦！」這位「臭屁仔」（我和蔡先生互稱「臭屁仔」），他就是愛虧我啦！

說到和大家分享古文物的美，我是十分樂意的。像我這樣一個從南部上來台北的鄉下人，今天有些小小成就，還有能力收藏一些骨董文物，大家也願意成全小兒宗明的心願，在我做七十歲生日前夕，在歷史博物館這樣一個國家文化重鎮，幫忙把這個聯展辦起來，我是個「土直人」，心裡真的只有「感謝」兩個字。感謝收藏家的支持和所有幫忙的人，也感謝大家接受「爽伯」的邀請，來看看「所寶惟賢」爽伯文物鑑賞展。

吳先旺

me how to get started in the collection of ancient artifacts, the one who opened my eyes
and showed me what fine objects truly are. Before this exhibition, he also came to my
house to help me choose the exhibition pieces. Tsai Chen-Yang is a respected elder in the
antique collection world, but he carefully and respectfully looked over the collection for
six hours. He even laughingly said, "Uncle Shuang, your collection is so big, why don'
t you open an antique store?" This "old fart" (this is how Tsai Chen-Yang and I refer to
each other) just loves to pick on me!

I am extremely happy to be able to share the beauty of ancient artifacts with the public.
For a country boy from the south like me to have this kind of small accomplishment and
the ability to collect these ancient artifacts, and for everyone to grant the wish of my
son Zong-Ming to put together this joint exhibition at the palace of Chinese culture, the
National Museum of History, all I can say is that I feel "gratitude." I am thankful for the
support of all the collectors and all the people who have helped. I am also thankful for
all the people who have accepted Uncle Shuang's invitation to view this "A Sage's Respect
for Artistic Treasures—An Exhibition of Uncle Shuang's Collection."

**Wu Xian-Wang**

# One Dollar's Worth of Noodles
# Made Me Think for Fifty-five Years

Fifty-five years ago, when I had just come up to Taipei from the south to work as a mechanic in a motorcycle shop, my monthly pay didn't amount to much, and I had to be tight with my spending since I had to send money back home. On one occasion during that time, my co-worker, Liu Hong-Ru, who later became the owner of Tai Yi Motorcycle Shop (and is currently the director of the Taipei City Motorcycle Shop Federation), treated me to a simple bowl of noodles. At that time, I was so poor that I used to have to skip meals, so that bowl of noodles seemed amazingly expensive to me.

That happened such a long time ago, so why would I be thinking about that bowl of noodles on the eve of the "A Sage's Respect for Artistic Treasures" exhibition at the National Museum of History?

It's because I was thinking about the taste of "gratitude." In my tough "rags to riches" life, none of the good things that have happened to me came easily, and I have many people to thank for making them come true.

My son Zong-Ming wished to give me a meaningful 70th birthday, so he invited friends in the collecting world to hold a collection exhibition for me. This is what made me think of the taste of "gratitude."

I remember when Director Huang Yong-Chuan and Associate Director Gao Yu-Zhen of the National Museum of History came to my house with researchers and experts to see my collection. Although it was my house, I had to stand back without making any comments to give the experts some space to make observations and judgments. From afar, I could see the experts taking out their rulers and recording their notes. They were immersed in discussion and had serious looks on their faces. I felt full of respect for them and thought, "These people are professionals." My feeling upon having them take my collection of ancient artifacts seriously was one of "gratitude."

There is someone who was very important in making this exhibition happen, and that is Tsai Chen-Yang, the owner of My Humble House Art Gallery. He is the one who taught

# 從「沒有文化」到「所寶惟賢」
## ——寫在老爸史博館「爽伯文物鑑賞展」之前

清晨五點，我揉揉惺忪的眼，看見一個熟悉的側影，出現在暈黃的燈光下。

燈下的人，正拿著放大鏡，就著燈光，聚精會神地看著。他手上拿的，是一件玉器，這件美麗的老東西，穿越三百多年時光，從乾隆王朝的紫禁城，來到二十一世紀的台北外雙溪，靜靜躺在他手裡。「Magic Hour」。這是他和老寶貝獨處的「神奇時刻」。老爸像頑童一樣的好奇心和求知慾，始終是元氣十足的。今年，他要過七十歲生日了。

## 「沒有文化」，一切的起點

我應該如何描述我父親的收藏呢？我想就從「沒有文化」開始吧！

民國七十年，我們搬了新家，用力的裝潢了一番，請一位金融界的朋友到家裡參觀，人家客氣的支支吾吾了半天才說實話，「你們家景觀好，裝潢也不錯，不過在外雙溪這樣一個有文化的地方，你們家卻……沒文化。」

「沒文化」，這真是一下說中了老爸的傷心處。

人家沒冤枉他，當年，他還真是「沒文化」。

誰願意自己「沒文化」？對一個出身赤貧、窮到沒飯吃的窮鬼，不管是不是天才，都是「欠栽培」的野草，靠自己赤手空拳打拚出一片天，文化？對一個幾乎是文盲的人，不是奢侈，是連想都沒想過。

老爸真的被刺激到了。但其實這是一個美好的起點，「沒文化？好啊，那我就栽培自己有文化！」

他不買則已，要買就買最好的，所以第一次出手，就花幾十萬元買了一幅張大千的水墨畫，掛在新家那空蕩蕩的牆上。這幅畫像有魔法一樣，果然讓我們家變得「氣質大好」。

他以前不曉得「文化」是什麼，一個窮孩子潛伏的美學基因，直到五十歲才偶然被觸發，但好作品的力量直達人心，再鐵齒的人也會感動。老爸收藏文物的瘋狂「症頭」，就這麼發作了。

## 爽伯，也有繳「學費」的時候⋯

古文物收藏界都知道，這一行，剛入門是要「繳學費」的。那個「學費」，就是看走眼、買錯東西。

初期，老爸也曾經經過一陣入門的「亂收期」。有一天，他興沖沖地帶著一塊玉，請老朋友「寒舍」主人蔡辰洋「看一下」，不無「現寶」的意思。但蔡辰洋看了，輕輕往旁一推，就念了老爸幾句：「你不要亂買啦，要買就買最好的。」過幾天就帶老爸看幾件真正的「收藏級」好玉。這一下，老爸又大受刺激了。

看過好東西，開了眼，就真的回不了頭了。老爸決定，沒錯，要買就買最好的。從此，唯有百分百確定的好東西才下手，心裡有一絲猶豫就暫緩，他相信那份直覺一定有深意。遇到真正的好東西，他也會反覆確認，拿去四處請教各領域高手，譬如雜項和田黃他會拿去請教蔡辰洋，認真聽行家建議。

而老爸自己更是用功到不行。他這樣一個大字不識幾個的文盲，能不靠古董書、全憑實際的眼看、手摸、請教專家，從看好東西的經驗中累積功力，尤其是老爸相當自許的「識人」能力，他從商場上累積的敏銳觀察力，也運用在古文物收藏上，他說「我也許不知道東西是不是真的，但可以確定賣東西的人有沒有騙人。」

有人說，這叫「nature eye」，天生的好眼力。我同意這個說法，老爸少年「欠栽培」，但他似乎天生對好東西有種感應力，事實證明，除了判別真偽有一套，老爸還有種奇妙的鑑賞力，他收的宮廷文物，幾乎都非常優雅而有人文氣質，這跟他那一大堆人家認為「俗擱有力」的廣告，完全聯想不到一起，雅俗之間，落差實在太誇張了。

# 「會賺錢的骨董，就是好骨董」

不過，即使收藏了這麼多優雅的文物，老爸的「收藏語錄」，還是常令人聽了下巴掉下來，因為他一點都不故作高雅，甚至還滿有種「俗擱有力」的黑色幽默，譬如說，有人問他什麼是「好骨董」？他的答案是，簡單：「會賺錢的骨董，就是好骨董；不會賺錢的骨董，就是爛骨董。」

我有時會想：「啊，老爸，你都不會假仙一下，假裝有氣質哦⋯」但如果會裝高雅，就不是「爽伯」了，不是嗎？他一直同時用兩隻眼在看古文物，一隻是文人之眼，一隻是商人之眼：他可以為古文物的稀有美好而感動，卻也不會被感動衝昏頭，「有沒有增值空間」是他最後決定是否出手的關鍵。

其實，我想想「會賺錢的骨董，就是好骨董」，是有深意的。首先；你得有眼力看得出好東西；

再來，你得有財力買得起好東西；最後，你得有魄力，為它未來的增值空間放手一搏。如果這樣東西

果真「會賺錢」，表示你「三力齊備」，算得上狠角色！

所以，老爸的口頭禪就是「買好骨董有三力，眼力、財力和魄力。」好眼力是收藏家基本功，一旦看準，他出手，可也是「比狠的」，甚至可以「借錢買骨董」，他十幾年前買乾隆朝「幽蘭白玉屏」，就是這樣，買骨董也是要幾分膽識。為此，不知被管帳的老媽唸多少次，但老爸硬是得意的說：「有錢買骨董沒啥米，借錢買骨董才厲害。」

# 「冷凍庫」裡，有顆台灣熱心腸

傳統台灣男人，嘴巴就是不甜。嘴巴甜的時候，自己都覺得尷尬。

老爸就是「這款人」。所以他老是很顛覆地，用有「市儈」之嫌的字眼來形容風雅的古文物，開口閉口「會不會賺」，但其實他賺的，多數是個「爽」字，因為他收進來的古文物，根本很少出讓！有一陣子，骨董界都喊老爸是「冷凍庫」，意思是爽伯買東西「只進不出」，一進我家門，就被「冰」起來了！

「你白天想賺錢，晚上想花錢。」以前老媽老是這樣唸老爸，她說的「晚上想花錢」，可不是什麼歪哥的地方，而是他晚上最熱愛的休閒活動：逛骨董店，買骨董！這也是我們家族記憶中，最美好的畫面之一。

這十多年來，老爸常在忙了一天之後，入夜，帶著老媽，後來連我也帶上，一家三口就這麼逛骨董、看骨董、聊骨董，偶爾也跟著同好一起吹吹牛。有時晚上帶著當天戰利品，或者店家要老爸「先帶去看幾天」的準戰利品回家。老爸興頭濃得很，也不覺得累，回家就拿起放大鏡開始細看刀法、雕工，這一看經常就到第二天清晨，幾乎沒睡。

老爸最瘋狂的時候，幾乎天天買，難怪老媽唸他。但他自有道理，常用台語説：「買骨董有什麼不好？不奧不臭、不消風、不失重，擱會賺錢。」買骨董會賺錢？二十年前很少人聽得進這話，現在市場卻證明他是對的。

# 「所寶惟賢」，「所其無逸」

早些年，老爸幾乎睡在玉堆裡，床邊隨手一摸，就是一件古玉，他最愛邊講話、邊盤玉，把一件玉器盤得像回魂一樣溫潤含光，彷彿有了生命。父子對話時，老爸手裡老是有塊玉盤著盤著，這已經成了我記憶裡的經典畫面。

在老爸影響下，我也漸漸愛上古文物，我鍾愛印章，尤其是皇帝的閒章、收藏章，也和老爸一樣，以清代為主。這次老爸「做七十歲生日」前夕，應邀在歷史博物館舉行的收藏展，展名叫「所寶惟賢」，就來自我和老爸一起奮戰收藏的閒章。

這是嘉慶帝的一組閒章，其中兩枚，一枚是「所寶惟賢」，一枚是「所其無逸」，語出《尚書》，意思是「所珍惜、所寶貴的，唯有賢人」、「所前往、所努力的，無有逸失」，莊重大器，有帝王家氣象，今天也可以作為企業主的自我勉勵。這組閒章，是我和父親聯手奮戰十二小時，終於從古文物業者手裡「請來」，這是父子合作的一次收藏記憶，我特別珍惜。

老派台灣人，做老爸的幾乎不會説什麼甜言蜜語，做你兒子的也是。「所寶惟賢」的意義，就算是你送給我和孫子小賢的禮物了。老爸，「七十歲的生日，全家祝你身體健康、生日快樂！」

吳宗明

Father was really stung. It was a good starting point, however. "No culture? Well, I'll just cultivate some culture in my life myself!"

When buying collector's pieces, he had to buy the best. So, on his first purchase he spent hundreds of thousands of NT dollars on an ink and wash painting by Zhang Da-Qian and hung it on the wall in the new house. This painting worked like magic and suddenly changed the house into a house full of class.

Before, he never knew what "culture" was, but there was an aesthetics gene in that son of a poor family that did not develop until he was in his 50s. Great artworks, however, have the power to move anyone, even the toughest of men. This is how father's obsession with collecting cultural artifacts started.

## Uncle Shuang Also Had to Pay His "Dues"

People in the ancient artifact collection world know that you are required to pay your "dues" to enter this business. These "dues" mean buying the wrong thing because you are inexperienced.

In the beginning, Father went though that period of paying "arbitrary fees" that beginners have to go through. One day, he impulsively brought a piece of jade to his friend Tsai Chen-Yang, the owner of My Humble House Art Gallery, for him to examine, though he was also showing off his treasure. When Tsai Chen-Yang looked at it, he gently pushed it aside and said to my father: "Don't buy random things. If you're going to buy something, then buy the best." A few days later, he took my father to see a few real "collector's level" pieces of fine jade. This was another shock to my Father's system.

After seeing some fine pieces, he got a new perspective, and there was no turning back from there. Father decided that, indeed, if you're going to buy something, then buy the best. Since then, he only bought something when he was 100% sure of its value. If he had the slightest hesitation or desire to put off the purchase, he saw that as a true sign that his instinct was trying to tell him something. When he came across something truly fine, he would get separate confirmations, taking it around to various experts. He would take Hetian jade, for example, to Tsai Chen-Yang and seriously listen to his expert opinion.

# From "No Culture" to "A Sage's Respect for Artistic Treasures"

—In Anticipation of My Father's "Exhibition of Uncle Shuang's Collection" at the Museum of History

At 5:00 in the morning, I rubbed my sleepy eyes and saw a familiar silhouette appear in the dim light.

The person in the light was holding a magnifying glass and concentrating on something. He held a piece of jade that had journeyed from Qianlong's court over 300 years ago to 21st century Taipei . It was the "magic hour" in which he spent time alone with his treasures. Father has the curiosity and thirst for knowledge of a child, and he will celebrate his 70th birthday this year.

## "No Culture" Was the Starting Point

How can I describe my father's collection? I have to start from "no culture."

When our family moved in 1981, we put a lot of effort into decorating the new house. My father invited a friend in the financial industry to our house, and this friend politely stammered for a while and then said what he really thought: "Your house has a nice landscaping and the decorations are good, but for a house in a cultural district like Waishuanghsi, your house has... no culture."

The phrase "no culture" really hurt my father.

That friend wasn't slandering him because at that time, he really had "no culture."

Who wants to have "no culture"? What is culture to someone who was born in poverty, so poor that there was no food on the table, a possible genius who flourished without the proper cultivation and who built his own empire with his bare hands? For someone who was barely even literate, culture was not a luxury; it was something that never even occurred to him.

to have the wealth to be able to afford fine objects. Finally, you have to have the boldness to bet on its future value appreciation. If a fine object really can "earn money," it shows that you have mastered all three areas and you really have a sharp eye!

My father's motto, therefore, has always been, "There are three abilities to master in buying fine objects: a good eye, wealth, and boldness." A good eye is the basic skill of a collector. When he sees something he likes, he acts, sometimes being quite aggressive or even borrowing money to buy the antiques. This was the case when he bought a Qianlong "orchid white jade screen" decades ago, requiring a mix of daring and good judgment. Mother managed the books, and often scolded him but he always said with satisfaction, "Buying antiques with your own money is nothing. Buying antiques with someone else's money takes skill."

## There is a Warm Taiwanese Heart Inside the "Freezer"

The traditional Taiwanese male does not indulge in sweet words. When he has to say something elegant, he feels a little awkward.

Father is that kind of person. He always searches for the right words to describe his elegant artifacts, using the words of the marketplace. He often asks whether something will earn money, but what he is actually earning is happiness, since he has rarely ever tried to sell any of the artifacts that come into his collection! At one time, people in the collector's world called Father the "freezer" because once he buys something, it never comes out again. Once it entered our house, it was "frozen" there.

My mother often scolded my father by saying, "You earn money during the day and spend money in the evening." When she said "spending money in the evening" she wasn't referring to some unsavory establishment; she was referring to shopping for antiques! This has always been one of my favorite memories of my life with Father.

In the last ten years or so, Father worked hard all day and then took Mom, and later both Mom and me, to go shopping for antiques and talking about antiques. Occasionally he would brag about his collection with fellow collectors. Sometimes, he would take

Father was also tremendously enthusiastic. Here was an illiterate man who learned how to collect the finest artifacts not by reading books about antiques, but by using his own eyes and hands and asking experts for advice. He was confident that his ability to "read people," which he learned from many years in the business world, was applicable to the world of ancient artifact collecting. He said, "Perhaps I don't know whether the object is real or not, but I can tell whether the person trying to sell it to me is being honest or not."

Some people call this his "natural eye," and I agree. Father didn't benefit from an education in his youth, but he has a kind of natural sensitivity for fine things. Putting aside the distinction of whether an object is genuine or fake, Father has an amazing ability to evaluate the quality of the objects. Almost all of his pieces from the imperial palace are elegant pieces with a rich, high cultural character. This is a quality that people who know him from his TV commercials would never imagine he could possess. The difference between his coarse business personality and his elegant collector's eye is hard to reconcile.

## "An Antique That Earns Money Is a Good Antique"

Even though he has collected so many elegant artifacts and my father's "collection record" often makes people's jaws drop when they hear about it, however, he doesn't act like a highly cultured lover of ancient ways, and he still has his down-to-earth, dark sense of humor. Someone asked what a "good antique" is, for example, and my father answered, "An antique that earns money is a good antique. An antique that doesn't earn money is a bad antique."

Occasionally, I said, "Dad, can't you fake it a little and act like you have some class?." But if he had pretended to be refined, then he wouldn't be "Uncle Shuang," would he? He has always used two eyes when evaluating artifacts—one is the eye of a scholar and the other is the eye of a businessman. He can be moved by the rare beauty of artifacts but not so much that it clouds his judgment. His final criterion for a purchase is always, "is there room for it to appreciate in value?"

When you think about it, "an antique that earns money is a good antique" is a deep philosophy. First of all, you have to have a good eye to select fine objects. Then, you have we finally convinced the owner to sell. This is a memory of a father and son experience that I will always cherish.

Father, as an old-fashioned Taiwanese man, you almost never speak with sentimental words, and I'm afraid your son is the same way. You presented the true meaning of, "A Sage's Respect for Artistic Treasures," as a gift to your son and grandson. Father, your whole family wishes you good health and a happy life on your seventieth birthday!

**Wu Zong-Ming**

his night's booty home or he would take home items that shop owners told him to "try out" for a few days. When Father got home, he would tirelessly pick up the magnifying glass and start to study the carving techniques and the workmanship, usually until the morning light.

When Father got obsessed, he would buy something every day. No wonder Mother scolded him. But he had his principles. He often said, "What's wrong with buying antiques? They don't go bad sitting on the shelf. They increase in value." Can you earn money with antiques? Twenty years ago, no one would have thought so, but the current market proves he was right.

## "A Sage's Respect for Artistic Treasures" and "Indulge in No Luxurious Ease"

Years ago, Father basically slept on a pile of jade. He could find a piece of ancient jade just by reaching out his hand. He would love to talk and examine jade at the same time, making a piece of jade sound like it had its own soul. A common scene in my memories is that whenever we had father-son talks, he always had a piece of jade in his hand that he was examining.

Influenced by my father, I have also developed a fondness for ancient artifacts. I prefer seals, especially imperial poetry seals and collection seals, and, just like my father, I mainly collect Qing Dynasty artifacts. The items in this, "A Sage's Respect for Artistic Treasures," exhibition to be held at the National Museum of History on the eve of my father's seventieth birthday include hard-won poetry seals collected by my father and myself.

This is a set of two poetry seals from Emperor Jiaqing, one of which is carved with "A Sage's Respect for Artistic Treasures" and the other of which is carved with, "Indulge in No Luxurious Ease", which are words from the Shang Shu. They mean, respectively, that, "a sage knows how to respect what is valuable," and, "a gentleman should not indulge in luxurious ease in his ventures." This describes a man of great dignity, taste, and kingly bearing. These days, it can serve as self-encouragement for a successful businessman. My father and I bargained for 12 straight hours when buying this set of poetry seals before

# 乾隆皇帝〈玉枕蘭亭〉與〈觀成紀寓〉

## ——並略說他的書法學習

前國立故宮博物院書畫處長　王耀庭

〈玉枕蘭亭〉（圖見展覽圖錄），木盒裝，盒蓋線描漆畫，王羲之（三〇三—三六一年）坐蘭亭中，據案伸筆於硯上，舐筆而欲有所書寫。亭下白鵝兩隻，悠遊於水上。盒四邊畫百合、菊；梅、竹；蘭、靈芝；荷。盒座四方作花葉紋。盒內裝灰青和闐玉八片，第一為題目：（隸書）御臨玉枕蘭亭；第八為底，正面五爪龍；餘六片為〈蘭亭敘〉楷書正文。字為凹刻，並填金。款：「乾隆己巳（十四年；一七四九年）年仲春月既望御臨玉枕本。鈐印二：古香、太璞。」此「乾隆己巳（十四年；一七四九年）年仲春月既望」年款當指毛筆寫作，這到碾成玉片，自然尚須一段時間。乾隆十四年（一七四九年）的《內務府各作成做活計檔》的記錄，有一處可參證：

（十二月）初三日。七品首領薩木哈來說：「太監胡世傑交〈御筆白玉玉蘭亭〉四片、〈御筆白玉五福德經四片〉，傳旨：著俱各填金各配紫檀木罩蓋夾匣盛裝，先作樣呈覽准時再做。欽此。」

於本月二十三日，員外郎白世芳將做得罩蓋合牌匣樣二件，持進交太監

1《內務府各作成做活計檔》，乾隆十四年〈廣木作〉。（台北：故宮博物院藏影本），第五百八十六至五百八十七頁。

胡世傑。呈覽。奉旨：「俱照樣准做。其蘭亭匣做勾道填金。欽此。」

於十五年正月初九日，員外郎白世芳，將〈五福德經〉四片，〈玉蘭亭〉四片、配得合牌匣樣二件，持進交太監胡世傑。呈覽。奉旨：「著交金昆將〈五福德經〉的道理畫稿，持進交太監胡世傑。其〈玉枕蘭亭〉亦照意思畫稿，先畫樣呈覽，准時再畫。拉道填金，欽此。」

於十五年正月十三日，員外郎白世芳將畫得照〈玉枕蘭亭〉玉冊面上花紋紙樣一張，持進交太監胡世傑。呈覽。奉旨：「照樣准刻，其邊上花紋另畫好樣，呈覽，欽此。」

於二月初一日，員外郎白世芳將畫得照〈五福德經〉的道理佛像紙一張，持進交太監胡世傑。呈覽。奉旨：「照樣准做，欽此。」

於十五年七月十四日太監胡世傑。傳旨：「將〈玉枕蘭亭〉四片，並〈五福德經〉四片，現配做的紫檀木罩。呈覽。欽此。」

於本日將紫檀木罩蓋匣二件，持進交太監胡世傑。呈覽。奉旨：「俱交如意館□。欽此。」

於十五年八月初六日商得□交訖。1

從十四年（一七四九年）十二月交辦，到十五年（一七五〇年）八月完成。此項記錄時間接近，但此

〈玉枕蘭亭〉卻祇「四片」，件數顯然不合。但製作過程，從交辦、擬畫樣、呈准、製作，皆交待清

楚，可讓吾人了解宮中的工作。

王羲之於晉穆帝永和九年（三五三年）三月三日，約集山陰名士四十一人于「蘭亭」，修禊祭，

宴曲水，即席賦詩，匯為一卷，由王羲之當場用鼠鬚筆蠶繭紙，寫下〈蘭亭敘〉，分為二十八行，共

三二四個字，文章與書寫，心手相暢，書法史上是最為大家熟悉的王羲之名跡。相傳王羲之書〈蘭亭

敘帖〉真跡，曾被唐太宗所得，貞觀間（六二七—六四九年）令從臣能書者摹寫，因此，勾摹佳本

傳於後世，又刻石以廣流傳，唐時已有石刻拓本。〈蘭亭敘〉自唐以後分為兩派，其一出於褚遂良

（五九六—六五九年。河南），是為「唐本」，其一則出於歐陽詢（五五七—六四一年。率更），

是為「定武本」；至宋之多，版本之繁已不可勝計。

為了流傳與保存，將重要文字「銘金刻石」這是人類長久以來的習慣。〈蘭亭敘〉或者說它

是代表了王羲之書法的象徵。王羲之被唐太宗（五九九—六四九年）譽為「盡善盡美，其惟王逸少

乎。」[2] 相傳王羲之〈蘭亭敘〉墨跡已在唐貞觀二十三年（六四九年）為唐太宗李世民所殉葬。也祇

能靠著各種臨本來了解〈蘭亭敘〉了。

標題既做《玉枕本》，對於〈玉枕本〉何所出？這又是眾說紛紜。一般的說法，見清王澍

（一六六八—一七四三年）《竹雲題跋》：

〈玉枕蘭亭〉有三本，其一見《太清樓帖》，序云：「唐文皇（太宗）

使率更令以楷法摹蘭亭，藏枕中，名〈玉枕蘭亭〉；其二則宋政和間營

繕洛陽宮闕，內臣見後有役夫作枕小石，有刻畫，視乃〈蘭亭序〉，只

存數十字；其三則有秋壑使廖瑩中以燈影縮小，刻之靈璧石者。今洛陽

宮本不復可見，率更、秋壑兩種，猶有存者。[3]

2 唐太宗御撰《晉書》（文淵閣四庫全書），卷八十一，第十九頁。

3 （清）王澍《竹雲題跋》，〈玉枕本〉條，（文淵閣四庫全書），卷一，第十九至二十頁。

《太清樓帖》刻於宋徽宗大觀三年（一一○九年），那這是最早的記載了，且說明是「楷書」。

元許有壬（一二七八—一三六四年）《至正集》記〈跋海朝宗〈玉枕蘭亭〉〉條：

永和癸丑迄至順癸酉，九百八十一年。蘭亭一帖臨摹展促，殆千萬億化身矣！本來面目寧不變乎。朝宗所藏，校予所閱，蓋唐臨之佳者也，第世無吳，卒不知綱之果似芮否也。4

此元代認定「唐臨本」出現了。

明代王禕（一三二一—一三七三年）撰《王忠文集》〈跋玉枕蘭亭帖〉，卻是談〈玉枕蘭亭〉最多為人引用：

蘭亭帖自唐以後分二派，其一出於褚河南（遂良），是為「唐臨本」；其一出於歐陽率更（詢）是為「定武本」。若「玉枕本」則河南始縮為小體，或謂率更亦嘗為之。宋景定間，賈氏柄國，凡蘭亭遺刻之在世者，鮮不資其玩好。此本後有〈右軍小像〉，且題曰「秋壑珍玩」，其賈氏所重刻者耶。」5

〈玉枕蘭亭〉出於「褚」、還是出於「歐」？有二說，而南宋末賈似道（一二一三—一二七五年）又有刻本，則說法如一。其後有所謂「臨江本」、「福州本」。

〈玉枕蘭亭〉俗謂「黑老虎」，隨興可翻刻拓印，細節考訂相當困惑。文徵明（一四七○—一五九九年）對〈玉枕蘭亭〉即提出質疑：

4 （元）許有壬《至正集》，（文淵閣四庫全書），卷七十一，第十四頁。

5 （明）王禕撰《王忠文集》，〈跋玉枕蘭亭帖〉，（文淵閣四庫全書），卷十七，第七頁。

〈玉枕蘭亭〉相傳褚河南、歐率更縮而入石者。按桑世昌《蘭亭考》備著傳刻本末，所疏不下百本，而畢少董所藏，至三百本，並不言「玉枕」，疑是近世所為。柳文肅云：「賈魏公家數本，如玉枕，則是以燈影縮而小之，豈此刻即始於秋壑耶！又秋壑使其客廖瑩中，參校諸本，擇其精者，命婺工王用和，刻於悅生堂，經年乃就。特補勇爵酬之，所謂「悅生蘭亭」也。今世亦罕得其本，余僅一見於沈石田家，精妙不減定武，此〈玉枕本〉，有秋壑印及右軍像，而刻拓亦精，豈亦出用和之手耶！余嘗收得一本，與此稍異，蓋又別刻也。楊文貞云：〈玉枕蘭亭〉有二，一在南京火藥劉家，一在紹興府，二石今皆不存，不知與此本，及余所藏本同異，要皆不易得矣！6

十三世紀，賈似道刻王獻之〈洛神賦〉〈玉版十三行〉，若刻〈玉枕蘭亭〉也順理成章。關於〈玉枕蘭亭〉的記載，雖不只上述所引，但說來距七世紀前期的唐太宗實在太遙遠了。

乾隆皇帝（一七一一—一七九九年）喜好「蘭亭」，著名的王羲之〈快雪時晴帖〉冊，就有一頁他所畫的〈蘭亭義之觀鵝〉。對於此〈玉枕本〉，乾隆於明仇英〈脩禊圖〉一軸，上方就是他「御臨〈蘭亭敘〉」。款識云：「乾隆甲子（一七四四）夏四月既望御臨〈玉枕本〉。」7 此外，乾隆對〈玉枕本〉，曾於丁卯（乾隆十二年；一七四七）嘉平既望，以宣德紙、楷書，臨〈王羲之蘭亭詩序〉一卷。時間與本件也接近。8 乾隆之與「蘭亭」，最為有名的是乾隆四十四年（一七七九），在圓明園綺春園西北部，「蘭亭八柱亭」的建立，亭改建成重簷八方亭。乾隆題趙孟堅（一一九九—一二六七）〈落水蘭亭〉「曾因八柱刻貞珉」句下註：

己亥年（乾隆四十四年：一七七九）春，以內府所藏虞世南、褚遂良、馮承素所摹〈蘭亭敘〉，及柳公權書〈蘭亭詩〉，董其昌〈臨柳本并戲鴻堂原刻柳本〉，余所臨〈柳本〉，並命于敏中補成全字本，釐為八卷，刻石題曰〈蘭亭八柱帖〉。今是卷孫承澤題云是唐石唐拓，宋元以來稱

6 （明）文徵明撰《甫田集》，〈題玉枕蘭亭〉，（文淵閣四庫全書），卷二十，第五頁。

7 《石渠寶笈》，（文淵閣四庫全書），卷三十八，第五十八至五十九頁。

8 《石渠寶笈續編》，（台北：國立故宮博物院，一九七一），第二千三百一十二頁。

9 清高宗《御製詩集》四集，（文淵閣四庫全書），卷九七，第十三至十四頁。

10 按就《石渠寶笈秘殿珠林續編》（台北：國立故宮博物院，一九七一）之索引計算，此為同事何傳馨先生提供，謹致謝意。

11 〈御臨快雪堂帖御識〉，《石渠寶笈秘殿珠林初編》（台北：國立故宮博物院，一九七一）第二千三百九十二頁。

12 《康熙起居注冊》（北京：中華，一九八三），二十六年六月初十日條，第二千六百四十五頁。

13 《康熙起居注冊》（北京：中華，一九八三），五月二十六日條，第一千四百八十五頁。

14 見國立故宮博物院典藏本。

為墨寶，益可見山陰真面目。唐石雖不可得，欲用松花玉鈎摹成冊，以永其年。9

回到本題，說本件的書風，還是先了解乾隆皇帝的書法學習。乾隆皇帝的書蹟，在故宮收藏裡，讓人感到隨處可見的自是古書畫上的題跋，其數量之多，不曉得該如何估計。以《石渠寶笈》初、續及三編著錄，乾隆臨書及題識內府所藏古人書蹟，從乾隆二年（一七三七）到五十七（一七九二）年，總計約七百餘件（則），這還不包括他對於單件書畫上的題跋。10 對乾隆的書畫創作研究，令人感興趣的是他在書畫上的因緣際會，而不是做為一代名家的成就。乾隆就自己說道：「非欲與文人競追摹能事，聊以志吾幾務之餘，亦不肯頃刻自逸耳。」11

乾隆皇帝的書法，在龐大的乾隆詩文裏，卻不見到他自述何時從何師作書法學習。學習書法是隨著啟蒙教育來的，第一課認字「描紅」，也可以認為是學習書法之始。不知乾隆作為「皇孫」時，授經時的一位業師：福敏（一六七三—一七五九年），是否有過對他基本上的書法影響？清宮中的皇太子教育是包含有書法課的，康熙皇帝（一六五四—一七二二年；一六六一—一七二二年在位）在位甚至還親自指點評定皇子的楷書，乃至於展示給大臣們。12 從年齡上來說，乾隆做為皇孫，依例六歲學滿字，十歲學漢字，13 在南書房受教育，自不外於此。只是無法得知當時學帖的範本是那一家？若從一般習帖上的楷書學習看來，乾隆還是以「顏體」為基本。如見於〈孝賢純皇后（一七三一—一七四八年）繡花卉火鐮荷包〉（圖一）上的乾隆戊辰年（十三年，一七四八）詠詩一紙，這是很標準的顏體字，即使是到了乾隆丙申（四十一年，一七七六年）刻於〈澄泥墨硯〉（圖二）猶是有顏體字出現。

就這一現象，本件〈玉枕蘭亭〉，也是「顏體」書風，時間也相當接近。可以理解是乾隆帝所寫，而非吾人常見的乾隆題識行楷書。《敬勝齋法帖》四十卷，為乾隆個人書寫叢帖，摹勒於乾隆二十年齡（一七五五年）奉旨。第二十一卷至四十卷為他臨古今人書。這最能看出乾隆個人臨習的範圍。從漢朝鍾繇，晉王羲之、王獻之，唐之褚遂良、顏真卿，宋之蘇軾、黃庭堅，元之趙孟頫、明之王寵等等。其中卷二十三，戊辰（十三年；一七四八年）年臨寫的唐顏真卿《自書告身》（圖三），14 比起其他臨帖是更忠實的反應出顏體書的風貌，也可以與前述同年代〈繡花卉火鐮荷包〉證明乾隆對顏書的用功。

對於乾隆皇帝愛好書法的興趣，完全可以確定。一七四七年《石渠寶笈》初編上諭：「朕少年

時，間涉獵書繪，登極後每緣幾暇，結習未忘，弄翰抒毫，動成卷軸。」15 一七五四年《御筆

墨妙軒法帖序》：「朕聽政之暇，翰墨自娛，內府所藏書家真蹟，無慮數十百種，展閱之餘，

手自摹寫，品評題識，至於再三。」16 這猶如他口中的皇祖：康熙。康熙對書法的喜好，形諸於文

字著錄的，幾乎和乾隆如出一轍。康熙五十歲生日時告訴臣下：「朕自幼好臨池，每日寫千餘字，

從無間斷，凡古名人之墨跡、石刻，無不細心臨摹，積今三十餘年，實亦性之所好。」17

乾隆皇帝對於他的「皇祖」應該是有一份欽敬之心。書法上也是頗有步趨。試以故宮藏《清蔣廷

錫野菊軸》探討。本幅上有康熙題七絕一首：「山花野菊喜清風，塞北烟光報嶺楓。無暑不知秋

氣至，數叢藥蕊放離宮。乙酉（一七○五年）秋日山莊偶成並書。」從書整體之丰神言，清朗

中不失健峭，用筆形態骨多於肉，其中若「花、野、菊、風、煙」諸字的結體與間架，應是近於趙孟

頫（一二五四—一三二二年）一格。

康熙在《清蔣廷錫野菊軸》這幅題詩的上的「偶成并書」（圖四）四字，和乾隆書寫的《清高宗

亡清三可汗手跡：高宗御筆書畫》，也有「偶」（圖五），看來祖孫的氣息真是相通。乾隆在雍正八

年（一七三○年），《聖祖仁皇帝御書題畫詩一卷》18 這一卷的裝箱上寫到《賜御書記》：「憶自

年十二時，隨皇祖聖祖仁皇帝駕往熱河避暑，朝夕隨侍，皇祖萬幾之暇，輒瀏覽書史，或親

灑宸翰，從旁竊觀，心慕而未敢以請也。皇祖顧曰：『汝愛吾書乎？』賜長幅一、復賜橫幅

一、扇一、皆持以告我皇父，實而藏之。」祖孫之間的書法因緣，不管出於內心的虔敬，或者門

面話，有此相似現象並不為過。

對於乾隆皇帝常見於古書畫的題跋，書風上之出處或者奠基何處？王羲之《快雪時晴帖》的影響

是相當深刻的，乾隆本身也確實勤加臨習。梁詩正（一六九七—一七六三年）等跋王羲之《快雪時晴

帖》：「我皇上好古敏求，萬幾之暇，精研八法，是帖心摹手追，不下數十百本，而聖懷虛

受，猶臨池未輟也。丙寅（一七四六年）春正，清宴是娛，復臨茲帖，御製七言斷句五章，

題於冊首。因副頁宋歲古潤可愛，更濡筆作〈雲林小景〉，傳示臣等。」19 又臣工奉勅跋〈乾

隆臨三文翰〉：「皇上萬幾餘閒，每當春風秋月之時，展玩不置，近年以來，對本臨摹，不啻

15 《石渠寶笈秘殿珠林初編》
（台北：國立故宮博物院，
一九七一），第二百四十六頁。

16 《石渠寶笈秘殿珠林續編》
（台北：國立故宮博物院，
一九七一），第八百七十頁。

17 《大清聖祖仁皇帝實錄》
（台北：新文豐，一九七八），
卷二百一十六，〈康熙四十二年
七月乙卯條〉，第十九頁。

18 《石渠寶笈秘殿珠林初編》
（台北：國立故宮博物院，
一九七一），第二百六十二至
二百六十三頁。

19 見〈快雪時晴帖〉原件上
第十三開。

20 《石渠寶笈秘殿珠林
續編》（台北：國立故宮
博物院，一九七一），第
二百六十六頁。

數十過矣。以此御書日進。」[20]乾隆本人於丙寅年（一七四六年）也寫到：「王右軍快雪時晴帖為千古妙蹟，收入大內養心殿有年矣，幾暇臨仿不止數十百過，而愛玩未已……。」[21]所說對於〈快雪時晴帖〉的用心是可以相信的。

目前無法看到乾隆對於〈快雪時晴帖〉的整本臨本，但是在〈快雪時晴帖〉原件的封面上就有乾隆所寫「王羲之快雪時晴帖」一行標題（圖六）。而這一行字正足以和原帖「羲之快雪時晴」（圖七）諸字比對，乾隆寫來是相當恭謹，對原件諸字的結體，也中規中矩的反應。比起乾隆多數被筆法所拘滯的此類風格，自是不同。〈快雪時晴帖〉對於乾隆影響之深，一比即知。

就楷書而論，前舉台北故宮藏〈孝賢純皇后繡花卉火鐮荷包〉內有乾隆附詩一紙，出於乾隆對孝賢皇后的愛意，一生不逾，至老思念，應無代筆之嫌。也讓後人知道乾隆的楷書基礎。〈澄泥墨硯〉顏體的字出現。這兩件的字跡比起〈玉枕蘭亭〉較小，因此筆的提頓、粗細、勾挑，就較〈玉枕蘭亭〉不顯著。

〈玉枕蘭亭〉，出於歐、出於褚，乾隆並未說明，檢視乾隆的《三希堂法帖》並無臨〈玉枕蘭亭〉，也就不知所出何處。上海圖書館藏有〈式古堂本玉枕蘭亭〉及明〈豐坊本玉枕蘭亭〉，兩本均是近於歐陽詢書風，而〈豐坊本玉枕蘭亭〉筆劃稍厚，看來乾隆臨本不相似。最為著名的〈宋定武本蘭亭〉卻藏在清宮。孫承澤（一五九二──一六七六）跋〈宋拓玉枕蘭亭〉：「……摹之，而以歐陽詢為最，詢又縮而小之為玉枕。當時刻之禁中，已極貴重，後人稱為『定武』者，此刻也。」[22]

乾隆〈玉枕蘭亭〉臨書，每片五行，每行的字數，除第九行原〈定武蘭亭本〉的「所」字，提為第十行的首字，第十行雖增此一字，仍然以「之」字結尾，其餘由字成行，積行成篇的安排是一致的。如第一行，「癸丑」二字，注於「峻嶺」之旁。原本中的「向之」也一樣的寫得較大，「悲夫」的「夫」，最後一字的「文」臨本倒無原本的誇大。「之」字在王羲之原本的〈蘭亭敘〉裏，每字變化不一。乾隆本「之」字固然步趨，如「極視聽之娛」，「之」字則成「長捺」。王羲之〈蘭亭敘〉雖云行書，還是以楷為主，而乾隆臨本，運筆楷意的莊重意更多。

第十二開。

21 見〈快雪時晴帖〉原件上第十二開。

22（清）孫承澤跋〈宋搨玉枕蘭亭〉，《式古堂書畫彙考》〈文淵閣四庫全書〉，卷五，第九十二至九十三頁。

就每一字的結體，最主要的特徵，顏體字的正方端整，在這一篇〈玉枕蘭亭〉還是存在的。字的體態，如第三板，從「一觴一詠」到最後「極視聽」，更顯出顏體的基礎。這也可從字裏多是回鋒，頓挫再出鋒，如「也」字，這是最為標準。相對的，因是遵從〈定武本〉，字裏行間的排列，較為錯落變化，比其乾隆的一般行楷書，也顯得一份沉著。這還是臨書的關係，所以也必然有〈定武本〉的影響。

〈觀成紀寓〉冊（見展覽圖錄）本件冊頁裝，崁玉片，鑲邊黃裱綾。封面木板刻隸書「觀成紀寓」四字。前副頁，右幅空。左刻繪填金泥雙龍抱「壽」。第一開，左右幅均隸書，凹雕填金。第一行「平定回疆三十韻」，餘每行八字，每版四行。後副頁，右幅刻繪填金泥龍搶「珠」。

〔釋文〕：平定回疆三十韻。

回疆入版圖，耆定叨天賜。內安絕外侮，寧居逮一世。幸且歲屢豐，雪山水不匱。霖亦弗致澇，疏流總無滲。是誠為樂土，萬戶生養遂。昔屬準噶爾，朘削愁其啻。滅準歸王化，賦十存其四。大臣司捻制。首曰葉爾羌。漢語寬土謂。次喀什噶爾，名初剏之義。其三即蘇閬，譯謂漢人字。自古斯產玉，山水殊次第。山者却居次。春秋各取之，水出實上珍，貢入賞其勞，豈虛役人力。剖璞至刖足，憼言己明試。烏什阿克蘇，飛峯白水瀅。小城凡十三，不復贅言細。亦皆有督員，或並或單置，烏什昔作亂，實緣素誠罪，葉爾羌高樸，嘗玉為私弊。是皆抵之法，大都治外域，寓玉敢犯邊，回民安寢食。然豈易言哉，初無擴土願，更屬羈縻地。總弗敢犯邊，竟幸開疆致。每因失反得，明公兩言蔽。心惟敬與惕，哈薩布嚕特，慎勿生奢志。三十年安康，方敢言成事，敬以告後人，莫非昊蒼惠。

又《石渠寶笈續編》記有〈御筆回疆三十韻〉蠟箋本，行書。文字是相同的，且此卷引首也用「觀成紀寓」四字。[23]

23 《石渠寶笈續編》（台北：國立故宮博物院，一七九一），第二千五百六十三頁。

清廷一向用心經營中國西北，對於回疆，自康熙、雍正兩朝就相當著力。乾隆二十二年（一七五七年）新疆回部伊斯蘭教教主霍集佔兄弟（？—一七五九年），反抗清廷，殺清政府派往南疆招服的使臣阿敏道及兵丁百餘人。清廷先命雅爾哈善（活動於十八世紀）征討，後另派將軍兆惠（一七〇八—一七六四年）率軍平定。二十三年，兆惠率軍進攻葉爾羌之圍。二十四年夏，清軍分兩路出擊，兆惠統軍自烏什進攻喀什噶爾，富德領兵由和闐直取葉爾羌。回疆遂入版圖。平定回疆是乾隆自命一生的十全武功之一。24

24 莊吉發，《清高宗十全武功研究》，（台北：故宮，一九八二），〈第三章·大小和卓木的叛離與回部之役〉，第六十五至一百〇八頁。

通常所見的乾隆題識書畫跋文，絕大多數是行楷混合的書法，用隸書頗少見，以今日台北故宮藏碑帖，其冊頁面版，倒也頗多使用小字隸書刻出。出自乾隆「御題」的部份器物，也可見到隸書、楷書的刀刻銘紀。這或許運用隸書的端重，又可在筆畫中作尖提圓轉，諸種變化，比起行書更適合使用在長遠流傳紀念性的物件上。台北故宮收藏舉世著名汝窯，就有多件是銘刻著隸、楷書。如《北宋汝窯青瓷盤》（故瓷〇一三九六二），刻有乾隆乙未（一七七五年）隸書御題詩；（圖八）另一件《北宋汝窯青瓷盤》（故瓷〇一七八五五），刻的是戊戌（一七七八年）御題楷書詩。（圖九）《觀成紀寓》冊〈平定回疆三十韻〉無年款，必然是成書於乾隆二十四年（一七五九年）以後。從書風上說，乾隆的隸書學習的來源，未能於他的詩文集得到答案。書法史的發展，十八世紀的乾隆嘉慶時期，正是考據學興促成金石碑版的研究，書風受到漢魏碑刻的影響。奇怪的是清宮藏品，並無世所謂的漢魏碑版拓片。乾隆皇帝刊行的法帖，也還是一向所謂的「帖學」。或許是以流傳的魏明帝時《三體正始石經》（二四〇—二四八）容易見得到，成為學習的對象。

十八世紀以前的明清名書家，成就上行草楷書遠勝於篆隸。明清兩代書畫上的「引首」可常見到隸書的題識。乾隆時期清宮也收藏當時名家如王時敏（一五九二—一六八〇年）的山水，乾隆皇帝見過王時敏的隸書，應當可以預料。此外，清宮也收藏鄭簠（一六二二—一六九三年）的一幅名作《書楊巨源贈馬詩》，朱彝尊（一六二九—一七〇九年）也擅隸書。這三人是否對清宮的書法有所影響，一時恐難斷定。檢視乾隆周邊的文臣，也用隸書題字，那董邦達（一六九九—一七六九年）的書風或許接近。台北故宮藏董邦達《丹壑長春》題此四字，（圖十）及《畫中秋帖子詩》上的所書的〈御製中秋帖子詞〉。（圖十一）董氏的書風，如說他「力學篆隸」、「善篆隸書，妙得古法」25相互比較，年代或有差距，基本的字的體態，確是一致的。君臣之間的交流，卻也少有知曉。《觀成紀寓》

25 轉引自（民國）馬宗霍輯《書林藻鑑》，收入《藝術叢編》第一集第六冊。（台北：世界，一九六七）卷二，第三百九十頁。

冊的書風，正如隸書的端整大方，加以經過琢磨，字跡的筆畫也顯出挺舉有力。明朝人隸書在筆畫的轉折處，出現與楷書相同的運筆，在這一件上也出現，或許說明宮中並未有碑學派的影響。

楷書〈玉枕蘭亭〉與隸書〈觀成紀寓〉冊，是兩件以乾隆書法刻成的玉冊，乾隆存世書蹟以行草書為多，兩件分別由楷、隸書寫刻成的玉冊，說明乾隆皇帝的書學淵源與各體書法的涉略廣博。

圖一〈清 孝賢純皇后 繡花卉火鐮荷包〉

圖二〈清 乾隆 澄泥墨硯〉

圖三 清 乾隆 臨唐顏真卿（自書告身）

圖四 清 蔣廷錫 野菊 軸

圖十 清 董邦達丹壑長春 軸 （局部）

圖五《清高宗 亡清三可汗手跡：高宗御筆書畫》（局部）

圖六 晉 王羲之快雪時晴帖 冊 （局部）

圖十一 清 董邦達畫中秋帖子詩意 軸 （局部）

圖八《北宋汝窯青瓷盤》（故瓷013962）

圖七 王羲之書（羲之快雪時晴）

圖九《北宋汝窯青瓷盤》（故瓷017855）

本文圖幅一、二、三、四、五、六、七、八、九、十、十一「國立故宮博物院藏品」

*They were inspected. The command was: "Paint the drafts for the Classic of the Five Auspicious Virtues and the Orchid Pavilion Jade Headrest for inspection, and then finish them when they have been approved. Fill them in with gold."*

*The nineteenth day of the first month of the fifteenth year—Official Bai Shi-Fang painted the Orchid Pavilion Jade Headrest and submitted it to eunuch Hu Shi-Jie for inspection. The command was: "It is approved for carving as is. Add other decorative patterns around the edges and submit it for inspection."*

*The first day of the second month—The official, Bai Shi-Fang, painted the Buddhist icon for the, Classic of the Five Auspicious Virtues, and submitted it to eunuch Hu Shi-Jie for inspection. The command was: "It is approved to be made as is."*

*The fourteenth day of the seventh month of the fifteenth year—The eunuch Hu Shi-Jie commanded: "Submit the four tablets of the Orchid Pavilion Jade Headrest, the four tablets of the Classic of the Five Auspicious Virtues, and the red sandalwood box for inspection."*

*This month—Submitted the two red sandalwood boxes to eunuch Hu Shi-Ji for inspection. The command was: Submit to Ruyi Guan."*

*The sixth day of the eighth month of the fifteenth year—The matter is settled.* [1]

1. "Record of Activities Inside the Imperial Court" (1749, Guangmu Workshop) Palace Museum collection copy. Taipei. 586-587.

It was commissioned on the twelfth month of the fourteenth year (1749), and it was completed on the eighth month of the 15th year (1750). This recorded time is close, but the "four tablets" of the *Orchid Pavilion Jade Headrest* clearly do not conform to it. The production process, from the commissioning, to the creation of samples, approval, and manufacture, however, are all described clearly, and this helps one to understand the workings of the imperial court.

On the third day of the third month of the year 353, Wang Xi-Zhi gathered 41 scholars at the Orchid Pavilion, holding ceremonies and writing poetry to be collected in one volume. He used a rat whisker brush and silkworm cocoon paper to write the *Preface to the Poems Composed at the Orchid Pavilion*, divided into 28 lines, with a total of 324 characters. The composition and the calligraphy are both flowing, and the calligraphy is a famous work that is familiar to everyone throughout the history of the study of calligraphy. The actual *Preface to the Poems Composed at the Orchid Pavilion* was passed down to the Tang Dynasty Emperor Taizong, and it was copied by officials in that era

# Emperor Qianlong's Orchid Pavilion Jade Headrest and Record of Imperial Accomplishments Jade Book

## —Including a Brief Analysis of the Emperor's Studies in Calligraphy

**Wang Yao-Ting**

**Former Chief Curator, Department of Painting and Calligraphy**
**National Palace Museum, Taipei**

The Orchid Pavilion Jade Headrest (see exhibition catalog) is contained inside a wooden box. The box's cover is decorated with a line drawing in lacquer paint of Wang Xi-Zhi (303 – 361) sitting in the Orchid Pavilion, preparing to write calligraphy. There is a pair of white swans swimming in a leisurely manner in the water in front of the pavilion. On the four sides of the box there are painted lilies, chrysanthemums, plum blossoms, and bamboo. There are also orchids, glossy ganoderma, and lotuses. There are flower leaf patterns all around the base of the box. There are eight tablets of grayish green jade and Hetian jade inside the box. The first one bears the title: Imperial Jade Headrest with Orchid Pavilion Poem (in clerical script). The eighth is the bottom tablet, and it has a five-clawed dragon on its front. The remaining six tablets contain the body of the text, Preface to the Poems Composed at the Orchid Pavilion, in regular script. The characters are carved in intaglio and filled in with gold. The signature says, "Sixteenth day of the second month of spring, 1749, jade headrest book of imperial calligraphy copy. Two seals: Gu Xiang and Tai Pu." This date — "Sixteenth day of the second month of spring, 1749" — was written with a brush, and it required a certain length of time for it to be rolled into the jade tablet. There is one record from 1749, the, Record of Activities Inside the Imperial Court, that describes this:

*The third day of the twelfth month—Eighth class official Sa Mu-Ha said: "The eunuch Hu Shi-Jie handed over four tablets of Imperial Calligraphy on White Jade of the Orchid Pavilion and Four Tablets of Imperial Calligraphy on White Jade of the Classic of the Five Auspicious Virtues, commanding that they be filled in with gold and matched with a red sandalwood box. Before making the piece, a sample is to be made for inspection."*

*The twenty-third day of this month—The official, Bai Shi-Fang, made two samples of the box and submitted them to eunuch Hu Shi-Jie. They were inspected. The command was "Model it on this. The Orchid Pavilion box decorations should be filled in with gold."*

*The ninth day of the first month of the fifteenth year—The official Bai Shi-Fang submitted the four tablets of the, Classic of the Five Auspicious Virtues, and the four tablets of the, Jade Orchid Pavilion, along with the boxes, to the eunuch Hu Shi-Jie.*

The words that the Ming Dynasty's Wang Yi (1321 – 1373) wrote about the *Orchid Pavilion Jade Headrest* have been quoted more than any other:

> There were two versions of the Orchid Pavilion after the Tang Dynasty. One is from Chu He-Nan (also known as Sui-Liang), called the "Tang Dynasty Copy". The other, by Ouyang Lu-Geng (also known as Xun), is called the "Dingwu Copy". Lu-Geng made the calligraphy smaller. In the Song Dynasty and later, many different people made copies of it. [5]

Does the *Orchid Pavilion Jade Headrest* originate from Chu or Ou? Another theory is that there was another carving by Jia Si-Dao in the late Southern Song Dynasty.

Calligraphy tracing is popularly called the "black tiger" because it can be done easily but is hard to match in detail. Wen Zheng-Ming (1470 – 1559) had a doubt about the *Orchid Pavilion Jade Headrest*:

> The Orchid Pavilion Jade Headrest was passed down by Chu He-Nan and Ou Lu-Geng in a shrunken version carved in stone. There are hundreds of different kinds of copies in collections, and some may be recent creations. Liu Wen-Su says that the jade headrest calligraphy originated from Qiu Huo, who had his courtier Liao Ying-Zhong carve it after the example of Chu, which took years of work. There have been other versions of this jade headrest book, but they did not survive. There were two versions of this type. One was in the collection of the Liu family in Nanjing, and the other was in the Shaoxing government. They both no longer exist, so we cannot compare them to the other types. [6]

In the thirteenth century, Jia Si-Dao (1213 – 1275) carved Wang Xian-Zhi's *Luo Shen Fu and Yu Ban 13 Lines*, and then carved *Orchid Pavilion Jade Headrest* in a rational and orderly way. Concerning the records of the *Orchid Pavilion Jade Headrest*, although there are the aforementioned quotes, the amount of time that had passed between then and the Tang Dynasty in the seventh century was just too much.

Emperor Qianlong (1711 – 1799) had a passion for the *Orchid Pavilion*. He even painted, *Observing Geese in the Orchid Pavilion*, in Wang Xi-Zhi's, *Clear Day after Fast Snow*.

5. (Ming Dynasty) Wang Yi, "Ba Yu Zhen Lan Ting Tie" in Wang Zhong Wen Ji. Complete Library in Four Branches of Literature (Wenyuange Edition), Vol. 17, 7.

6. (Ming Dynasty) Wen Zheng-Ming. "Ti Yu Zhen Lan Ting" in Fu Tian Ji. Complete Library in Four Branches of Literature (Wenyuange Edition). Vol. 20, 5.

(627-649). There already existed, therefore, stone carvings that copied this calligraphy during the Tang Dynasty. After the Tang Dynasty, there were two versions of the, Preface to the *Poems Composed at the Orchid Pavilion*. One was founded by Chu Sui-Liang (596–659, also known as He-Nan), called the "Tang Dynasty Copy". The other school was founded by Ouyang Xun (557–641, also known as Lu-Geng), called the "Dingwu Copy." By the time of the Song Dynasty, there were countless versions.

Carving important documents in metal and stone for the purpose of transmission and preservation has been an ancient tradition in human history. The *Preface to the Poems Composed at the Orchid Pavilion* can be said to symbolize the calligraphy of Wang Xi-Zhi, whose art was praised by the Tang Emperor Taizong (599 – 649) as, "the ultimate good and the ultimate beauty, even greater than that of kings." [2] *The Preface to the Poems Composed at the Orchid Pavilion* calligraphy was placed as one of the burial objects in the tomb of Emperor Taizong in the year 649, so that copies of the calligraphy subsequently had to be relied upon for study purposes.

2. Tang Taizong's imperial writings, Jin Shu. Complete Library in Four Branches of Literature (Wenyuange Edition), Vol. 81, 19.

Why was it made as a "jade headrest book"? There are many different explanations. They can be summed up in Wang Shu's (1668-1743) *Bamboo and Clouds Inscription*:

> *There are three copies of the Orchid Pavilion Jade Headrest. One is a Tang Dynasty copy of the Orchid Pavilion calligraphy by Lu Geng. The second is a Song Dynasty copy, of which only ten characters remain, that was found in the Luoyang palace and copied by court officials. The third is a smaller version carved in lingbi stone by Liu Ying-Zhong at the behest of Qiu Huo. The Luoyang Palace version no longer exists, but the Lu Geng and Qiu Huo versions still exist.* [3]

3. (Qing Dynasty) Wang Shu. "Bamboo and Clouds Inscription". "Jade Headrest Book" lines. Complete Library in Four Branches of Literature (Wenyuange Edition), Vol. 1, 19-20.

The earliest record was in the Tai Qing Lou Tie in the Song Dynasty, in 1109. It proves it was calligraphy in regular script. Xu You-Ren (1278 – 1364) of the Yuan Dynasty records in *Zhi Zheng Ji*:

> *It has been 981 years since it was made. Orchid Pavilion has been copied countless times! Its original appearance has not changed. It is the perfect work for scholars to copy.* [4]

4. (Yuan Dynasty) Xu You-Ren. Zhi Zheng Ji. Complete Library in Four Branches of Literature (Wenyuange Edition), Vol. 71, 14.

It shows that the Tang Dynasty Copy appeared in the Yuan Dynasty.

This Orchid Pavilion Jade Headrest piece uses the Yan script, showing that it was written by Qianlong. It is not in the running or regular scripts commonly seen in Qianlong's signatures. The "Jing Shang Zhai Calligraphy Copybook" in 40 volumes was a collection of Qianlong's personal calligraphy, copied in 1755 by imperial decree. Volumes 21 to 40 are his copies of ancient and contemporary calligraphy masters. This is the best example of the scope of Qianlong's personal study of calligraphy copying. It includes copies of the works of the Han Dynasty's Zhong Yao, the Jin Dynasty's Wang Xi-Zhi and Wang Xian-Zhi, the Tang Dynasty's Chu Sui-Liang and Yan Zhen-Qing, the Song Dynasty's Su Shi and Huang Ting-Jian, the Yuan Dynasty's Zhao Meng-Fu, and the Ming Dynasty's Wang Chong. Volume 23 includes a copy done in 1748 of Yan Zhen-Qing's "Certificate of One's Own Writing". (Fig.3).[14] Compared to other copies, it more faithfully recreates the style of Yan-style calligraphy, and along with the aforementioned "Embroidered Pouch with Floral Pattern and Steel for Flint" made in the same year, it shows the seriousness with which Qianlong approached the study of Yan-style calligraphy.

14. See National Palace Museum collection piece.

Qianlong's passion for calligraphy can be absolutely confirmed. In 1747, the Emperor wrote: "When I was young, I had a superficial interest in calligraphy and painting, but since taking the throne I have taken every opportunity to study and practice it."[15] In 1745, he wrote "When not governing, I take up the brush. There are so many calligraphy masterpieces in the palace that I can use to appreciate and copy. I have evaluated and signed many."[16] His grandfather, Kangxi, also had a similar passion for calligraphy. On Kangxi's fiftieth birthday, he told his ministers: "I have loved copying calligraphy since my youth, and I have always written more than 1,000 characters a day. I have studied and copied the calligraphy masterpieces of all famous ancient masters for over 30 years, understanding their essence and style."[17]

15. Shi Qi Bao Ji Mi Dian Shu Lin Xu Bian. National Palace Museum. Taipei, 1971: 246.

16. Shi Qi Bao Ji Mi Dian Shu Lin Xu Bian. National Palace Museum. Taipei, 1971: 870.

17. Tai Qing Sheng Zu Ren Huang Di Shi Lu. Xin Wen Feng: Taipei, 1978. Vol. 216, 19.

Emperor Qianlong must have had great respect for his grandfather, and he was inspired by him in the field of calligraphy. We will attempt to probe the subject using the Qing Jiang Ting-Xi Wild Chrysanthemum Scroll which is in the Palace collection. This painting includes a poem written by Kangxi that praises the painting. The style of these characters makes it seem as though Kangxi favored the calligraphy style of Zhao Meng-Fu (1254 – 1322).

Some Chinese characters (Fig. 4) written by Kangxi on this painting are virtually indistinguishable from those of Qianlong (Fig. 5),. showing that there was a common style shared by the grandfather and grandson. In 1730, Qianlong wrote an epigraph on the box containing the scroll, Sheng Zu Ren Huang Di Yu Shu Ti Hua Shi Yi Juan, to the

7. Shi Qu Bao Ji. Complete Library in Four Branches of Literature (Wenyuange Edition). Vol. 38, 58-59.

8. Shi Qu Bao Ji Xu Bian. National Palace Museum. Taipei, 1971. 2312.

9. Qing Gaozong. Imperial Poetry Collection. Complete Library in Four Branches of Literature (Wenyuange Edition). Vol. 97, 13-14.

10. Calculated according to Shi Qi Bao Ji Mi Dian Shu Lin Xu Bian. National Palace Museum. Taipei, 1971. Provided thanks to my colleague He Chuan-Xin.

11. "Yu Lin Kuai Xue Tang Tie Yu Shi". Shi Qi Bao Ji Mi Dian Shu Lin Xu Bian. National Palace Museum. Taipei, 1971. 2392.

12. Kangxi Qi Ju Zhu Ce. Zhonghua, Taipei : 1983. 1645.

13. Kangxi Qi Ju Zhu Ce. Zhonghua, Taipei : 1983. 1485.

There is an imperial seal in a scroll book by Ming Jiu-Ying that refers to the Orchid Pavilion. The signature says: "Imperial copy of Jade Headrest Book." [7] In addition, Qianlong copied a Wang Xi-Zhi poem in 1747, very close in time to this piece. [8] The most famous association of Qianlong with the Orchid Pavilion is the building of the Orchid Pavilion Eight-Columned Pavilion in the northwestern part of Qichun Garden in the Old Summer Palace. The pavilion was rebuilt as a double-eaved octagonal pavilion. Qianlong commented on a line of poetry by Zhao Meng-Jian (1199 – 1267):

*Spring of 1779—All of the calligraphy and paintings collected by the Palace that involve the theme of the Orchid Pavilion will be compiled into a book titled, "Orchid Pavilion Eight-Column Book". These are Tang Dynasty stone inscriptions that were treasured as great calligraphy in the Song and Yuan Dynasties. Fortunately we can see their original appearance. Although we do not have the Tang Dynasty stone carvings, we can use song-hua jade to copy them and make books for future generations to see.* [9]

Returning to the main topic, to speak of the piece's painting style, we must first understand Emperor Qianlong's studies in the field of calligraphy. There are many examples of Qianlong's calligraphy left to us in the Imperial Palace. There are over 700 examples in anthologies published between 1737 and 1792. This does not include his comments on individual paintings. [10] What is interesting about the study of Qianlong's calligraphy was that he came to calligraphy by chance, and was not the greatest artist of his generation. Qianlong himself once said: "I do not wish to compete with scholars in terms of calligraphy ability. It is just something I chanced upon, more like a hobby." [11]

In the collections of Emperor Qianlong's calligraphy, it is never stated when he started studying and from which master he learned. The study of calligraphy proceeds from wisdom being imparted to students, and it starts with tracing characters. There was a calligraphy master named Fu Min (1673 – 1759) who might have been Qianlong's teacher. The study of calligraphy was one of the subjects for a prince's education in the palace. Emperor Kangxi (1654 – 1722; reigned 1662 – 1722) personally evaluated the calligraphy of the young prince and even displayed it to the ministers. [12] Given his age and position, Qianlong would have studied Manchurian at age six, and studied Chinese at age ten. [13] We just do not know which calligraphy master the lessons were based on. On the basis of the customary process of studying calligraphy in regular script first, Qianlong's preliminary studies probably started by copying the calligraphy style of Yan Zhen-Qing. There is a painting from 1748 with Qianlong's calligraphy that follows the Yan style, and there was another painting from 1776 that also showed Yan style characters.

style of Ouyang Xun. The script of the "Feng Fang Ben Orchid Pavilion Jade Headrest" calligraphy is slightly thicker, so it does not look similar to Qianlong's copy. The most famous *Song Ding-Wu's Orchid Pavilion* was collected in the Qing Palace. Sun Cheng-Ze (1592 – 1676) wrote, of *Song Ding-Wu's Orchid Pavilion* : "Copies are mostly made after Ouyang Xun and shrunk in size for the headrest. At that time, carving it was forbidden, making it more valuable. Later generations called it 'Ding Wu'."[22]

22. (Qing Dynasty) Sun Cheng-Ze. "Song Ta Orchid Pavilion Jade Headrest" Shi Gu Tang Shu Hua Hui Kao. Complete Library in Four Branches of Literature (Wenyuange Edition). Vol. 5, 92-93.

In Qianlong's copy of the Orchid Pavilion Jade Headrest, each tablet has five lines. As for the number of characters in each line, besides the ninth line, in which the "suo" character from the ninth line of the *Ding Wu Orchid Pavilion* becomes the first character of the tenth line, and though the tenth line adds this character but still ends with the "zhi" character, the arrangement is exactly the same. The two characters, "gui chou," in the first line are flattened, and the characters, "chong shan," are placed next to "jun ling". The characters "xiang zhi" are written relatively larger, just like the original. The, "fu," in, "bei fu," and the last, "wen," character are not as exaggerated in the copy as they are in the original. Fascinatingly, in Wang Xi-Zhi's original *Orchid Pavilion*, the character "zhi" is written in a different way each time. Qianlong's "zhi" characters follow this pattern, as well. Wang Zi-Zhi's Orchid Pavilion mainly uses regular script, and so Qianlong's also uses regular script. The main characteristic of the structure of each character is the solidness and completeness of the Yan-style script, which is evident in this, "Orchid Pavilion Jade Headrest". The style of the characters is based on the Yan-style script, as on the third tablet. This style is done by retracing the stroke, stopping, and then taking the brush off the paper. This is shown in its most standard form in the "ye" character. In the same way, since it follows the arrangement of the *Ding Wu* version, which has more variations, it seems more serious than Qianlong's regular running and regular scripts. This is because the copying was definitely influenced by the *Ding Wu* version.

The *Record of Imperial Accomplishments* (see exhibition catalog) is a book of carved jade tablets with yellow silk borders. The cover bears the four characters, "Guan Cheng Ji Yu," in regular script. The right side of the next tablet is blank. On the left side are two dragons holding a "shou" character. When it is opened, the characters on the left and right sides are in clerical script, carved in *intaglio* and filled in with gold. After the first line, every line is eight characters, and each tablet has four lines. On the last page, there is a dragon holding the character, "zhu," on the right side. The following is a translation of the tablets:

18. Shi Qi Bao Ji Mi Dian Shu Lin Xu Bian. National Palace Museum. Taipei, 1971: 262-263.

19. See note 13

20. Shi Qi Bao Ji Mi Dian Shu Lin Xu Bian. National Palace Museum. Taipei, 1971: 266.

21. See note 12

effect that he had learned to respect calligraphy and painting from the example of his grandfather, Emperor Kangxi.[18] Whether his liking for the appreciation of calligraphy, shared with his grandfather, was truly rooted in a deep respect for the latter or whether these were just superficial words, it was a liking that cannot be denied.

On what foundation were the styles of the ancient painting and calligraphy that Qianlong saw in the palace based? The influence of Wang Xi-Zhi's, "Clear Day after Fast Snow," was profound. Qianlong himself often copied from it. Liang Shi-Zheng wrote of Wang Xi-Zhi's, "Clear Day after Fast Snow": "Our emperor respects ancient arts and practices calligraphy when he gets the chance. It is very close to his heart. In 1746, he wrote a poem for the front of a book of paintings. He painted a scene of a misty forest, and informed his officials."[19] The official, Feng Lai, wrote: "The emperor studies and practices calligraphy whenever time allows. The imperial paintings are increasing in quality and quantity."[20] Qianlong himself wrote in 1746: "Wang You-Jun's *Clear Day after Fast Snow* is a masterpiece for the ages. It displays perfect inner cultivation. It has been copied thousands of times, and it continues to give pleasure...."[21] This shows the importance placed on, *Clear Day after Fast Snow.*

Currently, there is no existing example of a complete copy by Qianlong of, *Clear Day after Fast Snow*, but there is a title written on, *Clear Day after Fast Snow*, by Qianlong (Fig. 6). Compared to the title on the original (Fig. 7), Qianlong's calligraphy is very faithful and orderly. Its style is different from various other examples of Qianlong's calligraphy. It shows what a profound influence, *Clear Day after Fast Snow*, had on Qianlong.

Concerning regular script, there is an example of Qianlong's style on the painting given to his mother expressing his love and piety, which leaves no doubts about its authenticity and is found in the National Palace Museum in Taipei. It shows what Qianlong's regular script looked like. Yan-style calligraphy appears on the Cheng Ni Inkstone. These two examples are in smaller script than the Orchid Pavilion Jade Headrest. The strokes, therefore, are not as clear as those on the latter .

Qianlong did not explain whether the style of *Orchid Pavilion Jade Headrest* was from Ou or from Chu. In Qianlong's Hall of Three Rarities, there is no copy of Ou's *Orchid Pavilion Jade Headrest*, so it is hard to compare. The two pieces, "Shi Gu Tang Ben Orchid Pavilion Jade Headrest" and the Ming Dynasty "Feng Fang Ben Orchid Pavilion Jade Headrest," collected by the Shanghai Library are both similar to the calligraphy

Usually, examples of Qianlong's calligraphy are a mix of running and regular scripts, and clerical script was rarely used. There are many examples, however, of small-sized clerical script found on carvings collected by the National Palace Museum in Taipei. Clerical script and regular script can also be seen on some objects that have Qianlong's signature. Clerical script's solemnity and variety is more suitable for use than running script on objects that are meant to serve as historical memorials. Many pieces of the famous Ru Kiln porcelain collected in the National Palace Museum in Taipei are inscribed with clerical script and regular script. The "Northern Song Ru Kiln Celadon Plate" (Palace Ceramics Number 013962) is inscribed with a poem in clerical script from 1775 (Fig. 5). Another item, "Northern Song Ru Kiln Celadon Plate" (Palace Ceramics Number 017855), has an inscription in regular script made in 1778 (Fig. 9).

*The Record of Imperial Accomplishments* does not include a date, but it must have been made in 1759 or later. In terms of the source of his calligraphy style, it is not possible to find the answer among his anthologies of poetry. In the history of calligraphy, the characteristic of the 18th century during the Qianlong and Jiaqing eras was the study of metal and stone inscriptions, so their calligraphy was influenced by Han and Wei Dynasty stele carvings. The strange thing is that the Qing Palace did not have any Han and Wei dynasty stele rubbings in its collection. The calligraphy copies published by Qianlong were still part of the so-called "study of calligraphy copies". Perhaps the "Zhengshi Stone Classics in Three Different Writing Styles" (240 – 248) passed down from the time of the Emperor Ming of Wei was conveniently available, and it became the object of study in a limited way.

The calligraphers of the Ming and Qing Dynasties of the 18th century achieved much greater results in running, cursive, and regular script than they did with seal script and clerical script. The prefaces to calligraphy painting in the Ming and Qing Dynasties often used clerical script. The Qing Palace collected the landscapes of Wang Shi-Min (1592 – 1680) during the Qianlong era, so it can be expected that Qianlong saw Wang Shi-Min's clerical script. In addition, the Qing Palace also collected paintings by Zhen Fu (1622 – 1693) and Zhu Yi-Zun (1629 – 1709) who excelled at clerical script. It is difficult to determine whether these three calligraphers were influenced oby calligraphy in the Qing Dynasty Palace. The clerical ministers in Qianlong's court also wrote with the clerical script, and the style of Dong Bang-Da (1699 – 1769) was perhaps the closest. The National Palace Museum in Taipei has Dong Bang-Da's calligraphy (Fig. 10 and 11), and his style was a classical study of seal script and clerical script.[25] There may be differences in time, but the style of script is essentially consistent. We are a little

25. (Republic period) Edited by Ma Zong-Huo. Shu Lin Zao Jian. Collected in Yi Shu Cong Bian. Vol. 1, Book 6. Shi Jie, Taipei: 1967, Vol. 2, 390.

*The Pacification of Huijiang*

*Huijiang became part of Qing territory as willed by Heaven. The kingdom is now at peace and the borders are safe. The natural resources of the kingdom are abundant. A large amount of rain makes the rivers flow freely. The people are prosperous in this fortunate land. The Dzungar people have been liberated. The Dzungar tyrant is deposed and banditry has been reduced. Their five cities are under the control of our ministers. The capital is Yerqiang. In Chinese it is called Kuantu. The next is Kashgar, which means first cut. The third is Hetian, which is translated into Chinese. It has always been a place of jade production. The jade in the waters is the best, followed by that from the mountains. It will be offered as tribute every spring and autumn. The tribute will require great amounts of manpower. Embezzling jade will be punished by the cutting off of feet. Aksu and Uqturqan have great mountains and clear water. There are 13 small cities, not to be listed here. Despite the presence of high officials, there was a rebellion in Uqturqan, and charges were issued. The officials of Yerqiang were engaged in jade fraud. It was illegal, and those involved were punished. The capital governed the outer cities with fairness. The people were full of respect and caution. Hasabu Lute was controlled, and no one dared to invade again. The Hui people lived in peace. At first there was no desire to expand territory, but in the end fortune prevailed and there was expansion. Isn't turning a loss into a gain a blessing from Heaven? After 30 years of peace, it can be said that this was a success. It is a warning for future leaders to be cautious and avoid ambition.*

There also is a document in Qianlong's hand recorded in the Shi Qu Bao Ji Xu Bian, written on waxed paper with running script. The text is the same, and it has the same title.[23]

23. Shi Qu Bao Ji Xu Bian. National Palace Museum. Taipei: 1971, 2563.

The Qing Dynasty carefully administered northwest China, and, starting with the reigns of Kangxi and Yongzheng, they started to make effort in Huijiang. In 1757, Hojajahan (? – 1759), a leader of an Islamic sect in Huibu, Xinjiang, rebelled against the Qing Dynasty, killing A Min-Dao, the emissary sent from the Qing government to southern Xinjiang, along with hundreds of troops. The Qing Court sent Yarhashan (1689 – 1759) to quell the rebellion, and later sent General Zhao Hui (1708 – 1764) to lead the troops in pacification. In 1758, General Zhao Hui attacked Yerqiang. In the beginning of 1759, the Qing government ordered in reinforcements led by Fu De. In the summer of 1759, the Qing army attacked from two sides, with General Zhao Hui leading the attack on Kashgar, and Fu De leading the attack on Yerqiang through Hetian. The result was that Huijiang became part of Qing territory. The pacification of Huijiang was listed among the ten great military accomplishments of Qianlong.[24]

24. Zhuang Ji-Fa. Study of the Ten Great Military Accomplishments of Qing Gaozong. Palace Musueum. Taipei: 1982, (Chapter 3: Muslim Insurrection and Battle of Huibu) 65-108.

*Figure 4: Jiang Ting-Xi (1669-1732) "Wild Chrysanthemum"*

*Figure 5: Emperor Qianlong (r1736-95) "Handwritten Inscriptions by Three Qing Dynasty Rulers"*

*Figure 6: Wang Xi-Zhi (303-361) "Timely Clearing after Snowfall"*

*Figure 7: Wang Xi-Zhi's "Clear Day after Fast Snow"*

*Figure 8: Celadon Plate, Ju ware, Northern Song dynasty. (inv. no. 013962)*

*Figure 9: Celadon Plate, Ju ware, Northern Song dynasty. (inv. no. 017855)*

*Figure 10: Dong Bang-Da (ca.1699-1769) "Spring in Valleys"*

*Figure 11: Dong Bang-Da (ca.1699-1769) "Poem on Mid-Autumn Invitation Painting" calligraphy with "imperial mid-autumn invitation text"*

ignorant, however, about the exchanges made between the literati of that time. The style of the *Record of Imperial Accomplishments* shows the tastefulness of the clerical script, and the characters of this script became even more powerful after they were carved. The calligraphy in the clerical script of Ming Dynasty calligraphists showed a similar movement at the turning point as regular script. Perhaps this shows that the Ming Palace was not influenced by the study of ancient steles.

The regular script, Orchid Pavilion Jade Headrest, and the clerical script, Record of Imperial Accomplishments, are two jade books that were carved using the calligraphy of Emperor Qianlong. Most existing examples of Qianlong's calligraphy style are in running script and cursive script. That these two examples show Qianlong's calligraphy in regular script and clerical script demonstrates Qianlong's broad knowledge of the different types of calligraphy styles.

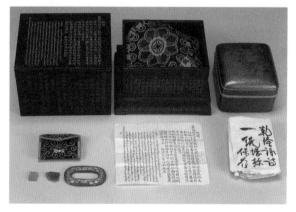

*Figure 1: Qianlong's calligraphy of "Empress Xiao Xian (1731–1748) Embroidered Pouch with Floral Pattern and Steel for Flint"*

*Figure 2: Chengni Inkstone, Qing dynasty, Qianlong reign (1736-95).*

*Figure 3: Qianlong's copy of "Certificate of One's Own Writing" by the Tang Dynasty's Yan Zhen-Qing*

*Figure 1、2、3、4、5、6、7、8、9、10、11 of the National Palace Museum*

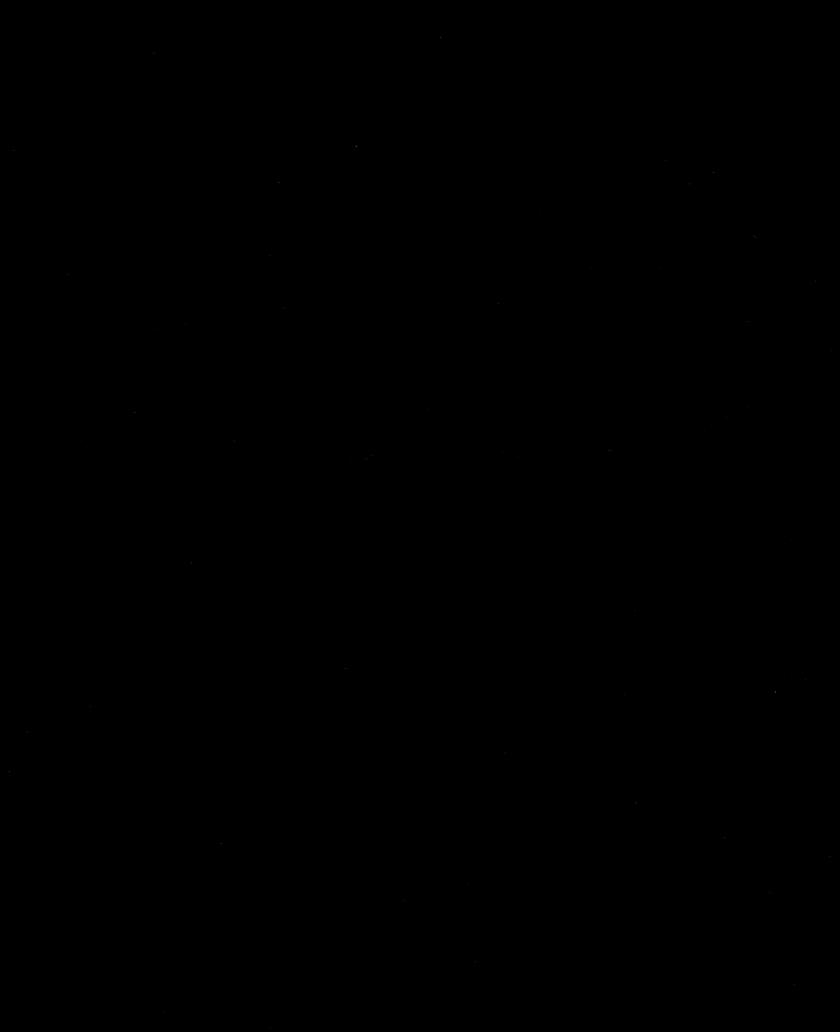

玉冊

## Qing Dynasty
## "Record of imperial accomplishments" Jade book

*L/14.5cm, W/7.4cm*

*Gray jade—made from mountain-mined jade into six rectangular tablets with text carved on all 12 sides. The contents mainly record conquering Dzungar in Huibu, resulting in the free flow of Hetian jade. Jade tablets were made to record great achievements of the emperors in order to report them to the gods. The script of the characters on the tablets is dignified and elegant. The characters are traced with gold. The front page is decorated with double dragon and longevity cloud patterns. The last page is decorated with a dragon seated on a cloud pattern. Each page is decorated with yellow silk, mounted in book-style, and there are sandalwood front and back covers. A four character inscription is inscribed and traced in gold on the front cover.*

# 清 《觀成紀寓》 玉冊

長 14.5公分　寬7.4公分　共六片　12面

灰玉質，係山料所製，作長方形板狀，共六片，兩面刻文字，共十二面，內容主要記載回顧攻得回部準噶爾，獲得勝利三十年，使和闐珍貴玉料可以順利取得，天下安康等事蹟之記事。玉冊乃皇帝祭祀天地山川時，為特別的重大事蹟稟告神祇所用。器面上文字，書法鐫刻端正優美，並以描金呈現，正面首頁有雙龍捧壽雲紋為飾，末頁則以雲紋坐龍為飾。每片加黃色緞料裝裱，並以冊頁式裝裱為書冊形式，再加檀木封面及封底，封面上有「觀成紀寓」四描金字。

御製回疆三十韻

回疆入版圖春□□□

先賜肉安絕水□□□

居遠式正率且歲□□

豐豐入水不竭其亦

井致勞疏源浚霖令

昆誠希樂土萬戶生

营遂咎居進寧兩胺

前殺弗害滅準歸土
化賦十存巨四其又
者五城大巨司徒制
宣曰某俞老漢語寬

王初聞斯
讚而譯産
次之讚玉
容義蹇函
仕奠心水
寫三字殊
廟即宣永
名穌古苐

水齒寶旦珎山者却
居次晉沐參取心紫
貢歷以歲貢入寶真
芳歲虛役以力十副

璞至知旦裏言已明
試言什四阿克蘇五
盛峯白水驛十城凡
十三不復贅言細亦

皆　豈　袁　薦
青　宗　誠　玉
智　什　菲　爲
員　咎　菓　禾
玫　作　爾　癸
竝　風　美　是
或　君　高　皆
單　緣　模　挺

之右此後眾知畏大
龍始外域明公兩言
敕然豈易言敕必惟
敬興惕叶哈薩布贈

特更屬羈縻地總并

敢犯邊回民安寢會

十初冊擴土願貢李

闕疆致宏因共反潯

莫非

昊蒼惠二十年安康

方敢吾成男故呂吉

後心慎勿生奢忘

# 清《御臨玉枕蘭亭》玉冊

長5.3公分　寬3.4公分　共4片　8面

白玉器作長方形板狀，共四片，可能作墨枕之用。上有乾隆臨蘭亭序文，字跡優美，刻精細。四片合裝於一長方形木盒。木盒為紫檀木所製，蓋面刻「羲之觀鵝圖」以描金方式表現，線條優美。

## Qing Dynasty
## Jade headrest

*L/5.3cm, W/3.4cm*

*White jade—made into rectangular shape for a total of four pieces, can be used as a headrest. On the top, it is inscribed with a text by Qianlong, finely carved in an elegant script. The four pieces can be placed together in a rectangular wooden box made of red sandalwood. The inscription on the box is traced with gold, with elegant lines.*

御臨盂校蘭亭

永和九年歲在癸丑暮春之初會
于會稽山陰之蘭亭脩禊事
也羣賢畢至少長咸集此地
有崇山峻領茂林脩竹又有清流激
湍暎帶左右引以為流觴曲水

列坐其次雖無絲竹管弦之
盛一觴一詠亦足以暢敘幽情
是日也天朗氣清惠風和暢仰
觀宇宙之大俯察品類之盛所
以遊目騁懷足以極視聽之

娛信可樂也夫人之相與俯仰

一世或取諸懷抱悟言一室之內

或曰寄所託放浪形骸之外雖

趣舍萬殊靜躁不同當其欣

於所遇暫得於己快然自足不

知老之將至及其所之既惓情

隨事遷感慨係之矣向之所

欣俛仰之間以為陳迹猶不

能不以之興懷況脩短隨化終

期於盡古人云死生亦大矣豈

不痛哉每攬昔人興感之由
若合一契未嘗不臨文嗟悼不
能喻之於懷固知一死生為虛
誕齊彭殤為妄作後之視今
亦由今之視昔　悲夫故列

敘時人錄其所述雖世殊事

異所以興懷其致一也後之攬

者亦將有感於斯文

乾隆己巳仲春月既望

御臨王枕本

# 圖說作者

清　《觀成紀寓》玉冊　林淑心

清　《御臨玉枕蘭亭》玉冊　林淑心

# Commentator

Qing Dynasty "Record of imperial accomplishments" Jade book      Lin Shu-Xin

Qing Dynasty Jade headrest      Lin Shu-Xin